ANIMAL KILLER

ANIMAL KILLER

A Novel
By B. Lee Baker

ISBN 978-0-578-44257-0 (Paperback)

Some Scripture quotations are taken from the Holy Bible, New Living Translation, copyright © 1996, 2004, 2015 by Tyndale House Foundation. Used by permission of Tyndale House Publishers, Inc., Carol Stream, Illinois 60188. All rights reserved.

Some Scripture quotations taken from the New American Standard Bible® (NASB), Copyright © 1960, 1962, 1963, 1968, 1971, 1972, 1973, 1975, 1977, 1995 by The Lockman Foundation. Used by permission. www.Lockman.org.

Some Scripture and/or notes quoted by permission. Quotations designated (NET) are from the NET Bible® copyright ©1996-2016 by Biblical Studies Press, L.L.C. All rights reserved.

Cover concept created by B. Lee Baker
Cover Design: mycustombookcover.com

This is a work of fiction. Names, characters, businesses, places, events, locales, and incidents are either the products of the author's imagination or used in a fictitious manner. Any resemblance to actual persons, living or dead, or actual events is purely coincidental.

Library of Congress Control Number: 2019900221

First Paperback Edition

Dedication

Dedicated to JC, JZ, TB, and the countless people who work on the front lines everyday saving, caring and protecting those who cannot protect themselves. And, to all those too many to name individually, who have played parts big and small in my life. My family, and the families that adopted me at times. To those who I properly thanked, and especially to those who I did not. To those owed an apology. Friend and foe. Those who stayed and those who left. Those who showed me kindness and mercy, and to those who did not. Those who I met and those who I did not, but yet still made an impact. I have come to realize that all the good, and all the bad, all the achievements and all the disappointments made me who I am. Without the tapestry of all these things, the impact of which is not fully knowable, this story would not have been possible. It is . . . divine.

Acknowledgments

My deepest appreciation and thanks to Jerry and Jill. Your encouragement and support made this book possible.

Tremendous thanks to my editor, Tom Cantillon.

Preface

My hope is that this story changes the world. Being a lifelong pessimist, I'll settle for changing a single mind. There are those among us who are cruel, dismissive or indifferent to the lives of the animals of this world. For most of my life, I personally never gave it much thought or particularly cared. In truth, I considered most passionate animal lovers a bit off-kilter. I no longer believe that. Now, I am one of them and boldly declare as a witness, one day the light turned on, I saw the truth, and was forever changed. Not changed in that now I simply care when before I did not. Rather, this new and involuntary act of caring fundamentally changed me as a person. It was a gift and a curse. A gift, in that I was able to shed the scales that blinded my ignorance and shunned God's will. It opened my heart, allowing me to experience love and joy like never before.

It was a curse in that my new found sight allowed me to grasp the immense worldwide suffering I did not, could not, see before. A suffering that once viewed, singes the soul. You have to force yourself to look away or be destroyed. Fully considering the problem, you realize it is akin to standing at the shoreline and trying to singlehandedly hold back the tide of a great ocean. This story is my small contribution to try to beat back that tide of suffering and indignity.

Whether you believe in God, or not, eventually we all pay a terrible price for the sin of how we exercise our dominion and control over the animals. If you believe in creationism, consider that God took the time to make the animals of this world, before He made us. He then bestowed upon us the responsibility to look after them. How can we possibly do anything, but appreciate, love and care for them? Like many theological concepts and dictates, God's will has been lost because so many of us rely on others to tell us what His will is. Despite what you might believe, or have been taught, the Bible commands care and protection for God's creation. If you want to know the truth, take a few minutes and find God's will there. It is not hidden.

In 2014, Pope Francis finally and unequivocally acknowledged that our animal companions have souls. We should consider the implications. It is not my intention to preach a sermon or thrust my theological understanding down your throat. I merely hope that you will seek the truth for yourself. One day you might find yourself standing before your maker having to answer for your time here. He might have a thing or two to say on this subject.

Gandhi said, in a time and place of great poverty, oppression and suffering by his fellow man that, "[t]he greatness of a nation and its moral progress can be judged by the way its animals are treated." He is right. They are our most vulnerable. Why do we believe their importance so small? With all of the problems of this world, many of us do not believe the plight of the animal to be important. For many of us, our minds are made up on the subject. When I find myself so convinced about my beliefs, I remind myself to consider what people understood before Mr. Columbus lost his way to the new world. For thousands of years they were all convinced the world was flat and that the crazy sailor was going to fall off the edge of the Earth when he reached the horizon. It was an axiomatic proposition. Absolute certainty. No need for debate or further consideration. We now know they were wrong. Seriously and fundamentally wrong. My hope is that we open our mind to the possibility that many of us are also wrong on this subject. Is it possible that God receives much pleasure when we show an animal kindness and mercy and care? I believe, when we come together and protect them, on that day, we will all be greatly blessed. If we do not have it in us to take care of one another, maybe we can all agree to take care of them and find some favor from their Creator. If this story moves you in some small way to help manifest any change like that, my life will have meant something. And, if not, at least where I was once blind, now I see.

B. Lee Baker
New Jersey
December 31, 2017

Part 1

For the fate of humans and the fate of animals are the same: As one dies, so dies the other; both have the same breath. There is no advantage for humans over animals, for both are fleeting. Both go to the same place, both come from the dust, and to dust both return. Who really knows if the human spirit ascends upward, and the animal's spirit descends into the earth?

–Ecclesiastes 3:19-21 NET.

The First Chapter

The sound instantly transported me back to a moment from my childhood. I was thirteen years old. It was the summer of 1982, Brooklyn, New York. I was playing third base for the youth league's baseball team. I take great pride in this because this was back in the day when you had to play well enough to actually earn a spot on the squad. Today, it's much different. Skill and ability have little relationship to playing time on a team. Nowadays, a parent pays a fee and their child is guaranteed to play and receive a participation award no matter how athletically challenged the child may be. Not all change is for the better.

I remember the day of tryouts. It was a scene to behold. There were hundreds of other boys with the dream of baseball firmly planted in their hearts and their gloves in their hands. Many looked terrified as they scattered about. I, however, entered the chaotic fray without much worry.

Brooklyn was no easy place to grow up, but it prepared me well for life and to play baseball under the harshest conditions. I had my friends to thank for that. They lived on my street. The neighborhood was sink or swim, not for the faint of heart. There were no parental coordinated supervised get-togethers in the bubble of their protection. Truthfully, most parents only knew what their kids did when something went terribly wrong. Luckily, I had the grit to survive and blend in. We played whiffle ball in the morning, stick ball, two street-sewers long, in the afternoon. Then it was *Ringolevio* at night. For the uninitiated, search it online. *Ringolevio* is a sophisticated team version of tag.

In Brooklyn, all sports, even baseball, was a contact sport. If you didn't keep your head on a swivel, you were likely to get beamed by a pitch or knocked over while running around the bases. All accidently of course. These shenanigans provided the comedic part of the game. It was half the fun. Everyone would get a good laugh each time someone would forget these rules and get knocked on his ass. And, for us, the harder the hit and longer it took for you to recover, the funnier it was. There were times when it took a good twenty minutes for my ears to stop ringing from a blow. There was no concussion protocol to protect us, and I am quite sure I played through several after being smacked down on the concrete. Oh yeah, we played on the street, not grass. There wasn't much grass in Brooklyn back then.

I chuckled as I watched these adults try to organize the crowd. It was easier to herd cats. Once they managed to create some semblance of order, the drills started. Fielding ground balls, running and hitting. All this in front of throngs of parents and spectators. Trial by fire. I have to admit, my experience on the street notwithstanding, tryouts for this baseball league was an entirely new monster to tackle. This was serious business. Bragging rights meant everything in this neighborhood. People watching and rooting for me to fail! My prior years on the street did prepare me for the ribbing I would receive that day, but it was unnerving hearing it from people I didn't know. There were times I wavered between wanting to run and hide behind my mother and wanting to take my bat into the stands and crack a few skulls. The relentless barrage of insults from the adults were worse than from the kids. Go figure.

The news I was selected to join the league came by telephone to my mother. I played it off as being no big deal, but I radiated with pride as I ran outside to find my friends, Anthony and Mikey, to gloat. They also made it. I knew they would. They were both bigger and better than me. Though, I would never admit that to them. My parents could care less. It just meant more money would have to be spent on frivolity. They preferred I get a job as soon as possible, or whenever legal, whichever came first. Work-age restrictions and child labor laws were a bunch of liberal gobbledygook that meant nothing to them. No one was going to tell them how to raise their kids. Children worked as soon as they could. No freeloaders.

After having been selected, I was even more convinced I was going to be a professional baseball player. Jimmy Devito from up the street was starting his first year in the minor leagues and a few other ballplayers came from the neighborhood, so why not me? There was nothing more fun than baseball. To be able to make a living and be famous playing a game under the shinning sun and blue skies, what could be better than that? Other than the day of tryouts, parents barely went to the games, let alone took a real interest in them. Again, it was all about the bragging rights. Parents had to work. Today, it's not about bragging rights and fun, but instead, it's all about the business of scholarships and parental delusions. Unrealistic dreams, believing they can produce a professional baseball contract for their boys through the sheer force of their will and determination. Sad state of affairs.

I was slotted into the pee wee division, the smallest and youngest in the league. I didn't care. At least I was chosen. Many boys were sent home the day of tryouts never to return. After a few games with the pee wee's, the powers that be realized the epic mistake they made and moved me up to the junior league with Anthony and Mikey. This was my first day playing with the big boys and I was anxious to prove the coaches right. The bleachers, on the day in question, were occupied by a smattering of parents and onlookers. It was on this rare occasion my father begrudgingly took me to the game instead of my mother. He knew nothing about American sports. He knew soccer and waited for the day Italy would triumphantly win back the World Cup. Although he didn't truly care about that sport either. Again, it was all about the bragging rights and national pride. America became his home, but Italy owned his heart. He came to this country from Italy with six dollars in his pocket and half a high school education. I was playing third base and watched my father stare stoically at something off in the distance. He was likely performing the mathematical calculations of how much he could charge to landscape the fields. He was a landscaper. It was a cash business. He was sporting the unclean and overgrown seventies disco mustache and had a lit cigarette dangling from his mouth. The burnt ash grew, but clung to the remaining butt, as he contemplated whatever it was he contemplated. The ash sagged, ready to fall and burn someone. That someone often times was me. I still have a mark or two from his accidental ash massacres.

I would yell, "Why can't you flick off the ash before it falls?"

His very practical response was consistently, "Why do I have to do it if it will fall on its own?"

He always smoked the same brand. To this day you can blindfold me and line up every brand of cigarette ever manufactured on the planet, if you light them all, I can tell you which one is his. That distinct scent will never leave me. I sometimes smell it in my dreams. He was wearing a white yellow stained t-shirt and tight, too tight, blue jeans cut into shorts. He decided to dress up for the occasion.

The other team taunted my friend Anthony relentlessly as he pitched.

"We need a pitcher, not a belly *itcher*. We need a pitcher, not a belly *itcher*."

None of us really knew what that actually meant. What is a belly *itcher* and why was it so bad to be one? We just knew it was us against them. It was us against the world.

The smell of cheap hotdogs, fresh cut green grass and the addictive odor of rubbing oil seasoned the air. The oil soaked our gloves. Any serious player knew you had to soften any new glove by rubbing the leather with oil and placing a hardball in the pocket. Wrap it closed with rubber bands and place it under the mattress. In a few short days you had a kickass glove that could be used in the field. That's how the pros did it. The odors left a distinct taste on my tongue.

The sudden and virtually simultaneous, *"whack!"* and *"whoosh!"* startled me from my daydream and my consumption of the summer scents.

It was the sound of a baseball being hit just right and then locomoting with some serious exit velocity, scorching the dry summer air. The ball sizzled as it blazed mortally close to my head. The crackle reminded me of the sound meat fat made when it dripped onto the glowing charcoal bricks of a barbeque. I swear I also heard actual voices enmeshed in that sound. As the ball whizzed by, the voices from within mocked and warned me at same time.

"Duck!" they cried while laughing.

Not very different from those twisted friends of mine. In the moment, as I hit the deck, and just before my face landed firmly half on the grass, half on the dirt, I recall thinking kids my age should not be able to hit a ball that hard. I immediately and painfully realized, despite having held my own with the pee wees, I was clearly out of my league. This too was not something I would ever admit publicly, but I knew it in that moment. As I lay there, I reconsidered my future career choice. I could not fathom how much harder a professional could hit the ball than the one that almost ended me.

I would never go on to play baseball professionally. In fact, I would never play hard baseball again. I would limit my sporting activities to whiffle and stick ball on the street every now and again. It seemed life had other plans for me. After witnessing my poor attempt at playing third base, my father decided I would work with him in the summer.

"*Ehh*, what's the difference?" He would ask. "You're outside doing stuff under the sun. Same thing."

He didn't get it. I slowly stood, spitting both dirt and grass from my mouth. The sight of this only intensified the jeers and uncontrollable laughter from my new sworn enemies in the visiting dugout.

Animal Killer

Mikey and Anthony, along with the rest of my teammates, had trouble holding back their own laughter. This only encouraged the taunting. The devil's minions craftily at work. The gush of adrenaline exploded into my face, turning it warm and fiery red. These clowns thought the near miss of my sudden and ultimate demise was a real riot. I was almost killed in the prime of my baseball career, and for them, this was the comedy hour. Such was life in Brooklyn. There were no safe places from the ruthless taunting and ribbing. It built character. You had to learn how to dish it out as much as you had to take it to survive.

The look on my father's face said it all. He was far from pleased. At least he was watching. He was trying to figure out how the hell he allowed my mother and me to convince him to shell out the thirty dollars for a glove, forty dollars for the league and the additional rental fee for the uniform. None of which we could afford, he would claim. Another wasted endeavor. But he was old school and thought about throwing a real beating to those kids laughing at me. I was thankful for that mindset. It help distract him from his typical first urge, which would have been to throw me a beating for wasting his time and money. An outcome not entirely out of the question, notwithstanding his disgust for those laughing. Child protective services didn't have the cachet back then that they have today. When I was growing up, a parent could throw a kid a beating once in a while and not land himself in jail. It helped keep the order of things. A good beating every now and again helped define the hierarchy of the family and community. It made things clear and maintained everyone's expectations. Children were born and continued to exist at the whim and pleasure of the parent. Quite different from today. Today, the inmates run the asylum. Lucky for me, I was no worse for the wear. The hit that almost ended me turned into a double. In the end, we would win the game. But, I was done.

I had not thought of that moment since. Not until this very minute. At least not to that level of detail. It would not be a small coincidence. Amazing how a simple sound combination triggered all those memories and particulars in an instant. That "*whack*" and "*whoosh*" combination. They say certain smells can trigger memories. I guess certain sounds can as well. Today, some thirty five years later, I am not that same little boy getting laughed at on that warm day. It's not the summer of my youth, but the cold cruelty of adulthood. The world had grown meaner and so had I.

Animal Killer

After that last summer of baseball, which ended with me working with my father for his landscaping business, he began to teach me to hunt. It was a difficult process. But, hunting was in my family's DNA. At least that's what he declared to me several times. My father was determined to pass this legacy on to me. He was no nonsense. It had been his teaching that lead me to this day in the mountains in upstate New York. From that day forward, my father taught me how to shoot and kill animals. It took some coaxing at first, but it eventually stuck, and I got hooked. I've been doing it ever since.

Years later, I taught my son to hunt, as my father had taught me. To keep the tradition alive, once every year, my son and I would hunt together. These were good times. Then a few years ago, I started a similar ritual with the top billing attorneys in my office, inviting them to join me and my son to hunt in these mountains. One long weekend a year we would take this pilgrimage to have a friendly competition to see who could bring down the biggest buck. It was on the last one of these extended outings where I would hear that familiar sound. I was alone. We all agreed to spread out and go our own way. This made the competition fair.

I panted as I forced my way through three feet of heavy snow, slipping on the ice that lie beneath. The wind bit at my face. It was unforgiving. Many things would be unforgiving this day. The hills and the creek were frozen solid. The air stabbed at my lungs. Breathing too hard caused a similar effect of breathing in menthol. It had that certain sting to it. It was awesome. I am not too humble to share that I had compiled a string of wins several years running, having scored the biggest bucks. Through my father's tutelage and practice I became quite skilled at it and earned my nickname, Animal Killer. Coworkers around the office called me by it. The moniker was banded about as a euphemism for my trial tactics. Colleagues would say, *Oh those poor bastards are going to have to go up against the Animal Killer.* I went with it. I even created a social media page, and rather than use my name, I simply called myself, Animal Killer. I also ordered personalized license plates for my truck that read, "Aml klr."

On this day, it was very quiet. I always loved how a large snowfall created a physical phenomenon of deadening the sounds of the world. It made the Earth very tranquil and peaceful, amplifying the feeling of solitude. Out here, it was man versus beast. In that moment, there was nothing else. I was making my way back to my tree stand while deliberately leaving behind a trail of deer urine. That was my secret. Each year, I bought a fresh squeeze bottle filled with the liquid waste. As I squirted the foul fluid, I wondered how they collected it. I made a mental note to ask the outdoor store clerk next year if he knew. However they gathered the discharge, it would give me a distinct advantage over the others, covering my scent, while attracting my prey. I quietly positioned myself in the stand and waited. Snow began to fall and I could hear the flap of the wings of the oversized hawk that circled above. I watched him fly through the snowflakes and assumed he watched me watch him. Without much effort, a doe wandered right under me. I thought she was a buck at first because she had antlers. But, upon further inspection, I confirmed she was a doe. This would be an uncommon kill. I watched her for a bit, and realized it was starting to get late. Today's kill was going to be her or return empty handed, and that wasn't going to happen. I took aim. She was dead center on the cross hairs and I was about to shoot when I caught her gaze. She fixated on two larger bucks heading her way. That stare would become the difference between life and death. Life seems so hearty, but the invisible thin plane that separates life from death that envelopes us all, is unquestionably quite frail. A simple gaze would save that doe's life. I relaxed my finger from the trigger. The animal would never know how close she came.

I waited to see what would happen. It was worth the wait. One of the two bucks and the doe began to fight. Smacking antlers. The smacking, cracking blows, briefly echoed before they were silenced by the blanket of snow. The doe, battered from the fight, ceded defeat and headed off. I took aim at the victor as he was the largest of the three and would surely offer me bragging rights. I counted his antlers. Twelve points. More points and grander, this magnificent kill would undoubtedly be the largest of our group. This one would allow me to claim victory again. After hours of anticipation, the moment of truth arrived. No matter how many times I had done this, the adrenaline gushed and flooded my veins. My heart pulsated so hard I worried it was going to explode inside my chest. My blood pressure increased causing my ears to throb with a heartbeat of their own. Unconsciously, I grinned. I took one deep breath and fired. The sound of the shot sent all three scattering. I was certain I hit the buck cleanly with a kill shot, but it too took off just as quickly as the others. I made my way down the tree and was surprised to see no blood. I followed in the same direction of the still walking, but what had to be dead, deer. Within moments, I located several droplets of blood staining the pristine snow. Still unable to locate the buck, mild panic set in. I felt pangs of guilt that the deer was mortally injured and suffering and that I would not be able to find it. Also, going back empty handed was not a pleasing thought. I had my rep to maintain.

Forty five minutes moving through the deep and heavy snow, following the animal's tracks and blood, I was drenched in my secretions and becoming increasingly uncomfortable. I made my way over a rocky hill and finally heard the beast gasping for breath. The gurgling sound of it drowning in its own blood. *Tough son of a bitch*, I thought to myself. Held on longer than any other wounded animal I had ever shot. I looked into the dead stare it offered and rhetorically hollered to the sky,

"Who's the man! Who's the man!"

This established not just my superiority over the animal, but my extraordinary tracking skills. The animal was clearly mortally wounded and I could just let it bleed out. I looked into its eyes and contemplated what to do. I checked my watch and noted it was getting late. I also needed something to drink and to get out of these wet clothes, so I decided to end it. I took several steps back, aimed my rifle, and mercifully sealed the deal with a single booming shot to the heart. I took out my selfie stick and phone to capture the moment for posterity. I held the stick in one hand and grabbed the antlers to twist and raise its head toward the camera with the other. I snapped the photo donning my shit-eating grin.

I thought about the events that brought me to this particular moment and place. The annual office excursion to these mountains traditionally took place in early December. But this year was different. This year, I booked this trip a week before the Thanksgiving holiday to coincide with the start of hunting season. I moved up the outing so I could escalate my yearlong, ongoing, bare knuckle, all-out, online brawl with an animal right's kook who found my online profile and decided to start a war with me. Bad move for her. The trip would offer me the forum for revenge and opportunity to turn the screws to her. It all started after I posted a picture of my son and I standing victoriously over a dead mother bear and her cub. The bitch, that was my nickname for her; her given name was Sandy. Sandy decided to call the law firm where I worked to complain that they had a murderer working for them. The bitch played dirty. With that, the gloves came off. I promised her I would provide her with more pictures of the dead. I promised her a killing spree that would not stop and that it would all be her fault. I knew that would get her going. In retrospect, maybe not my finest hour, but she really pissed me off. I was determined to live up to my nickname and told her I would take down one creature each day on my trip and post pictures of their carcasses online. I knew I would have to bribe a local official or two in order to get away with killing more than the one buck per season that was permitted, but it would be worth it. The bitch cried and called me a monster. I laughed. She should have spent her time worrying about people, not some dumb animals.

The sun that had briefly knifed through the clouds was quickly enveloped by some very dark ones; a quick moving snow squall was heading our way. My heart continued pounding in my ears and I could feel my blood speeding through my limbs causing them to also throb. The excitement from the kill and subsequent chase always did that to me ever since my father had taken me on our first hunting trip. It was barely above freezing, but I was overheated and soaked in perspiration. I had to get back inside. I was looking forward to sharing the impressive story of my conquest and declare victory. Given the conditions and terrain, there was no way to drag the beast back to the cabin without first gutting it. I propped my rifle against a tree and took out my knife. I rolled the buck onto its side and cut him from the sternum down to his genitals.

I pried him open and cut away at the fatty tissue that held his insides in position. His overheated entrails spilled out onto the fresh snow. They plopped out of him and sunk, melting the snow, causing steam to billow up and perfume the winter air. I then rolled him over onto his stomach and shook him back and forth to help the remaining organs and insides spill out. Once he was emptied, I took my knife and punctured his hind legs behind the Achilles tendons. I threaded the rope I brought with me through the holes I made and tied off the ends. This created a handle. I stepped in the middle and placed the rope about waist high and began to drag the carcass behind me. It was incredibly difficult because of the heavy wet snow and size of the beast.

I only made it a step or two when suddenly, I could hear grunting and galloping footsteps. They were moving fast and coming toward me, breaking the serene, snow deadened, silence. They were on me in an instant. Two bucks burst out from the cover of the snow squall careening pass me.

I let out a scream, "Fuck!"

One almost smashed into me, but in the last instant managed to contort his body around me. It happened so fast, startling me. I froze. Except for the sounds from the bucks, it was still so quiet, I could hear them forcing the cold air into their mammoth bodies. Sucking it in to keep them moving from their pursuing predator and ultimate demise. Probably being chased by someone in my party I assumed. Then, the explosion and the last sound I would hear in this life, that "*whack!*" and "*whoosh!*" I only half turned my head toward the sound when I realized what it was. But, by then, it was too late. The sound of the bullet cutting through the falling snow; buzzing like an agitated killer bee on the attack. The sound was eerily similar to that baseball that narrowly missed decapitating me so many years ago on the baseball field. This time, I was not as lucky. It didn't miss. My chest exploded and I collapsed to the ground with a thud. The bullet meant to bring down the fleeing deer.

I could still see, however, but for a constant painful ringing in my ears, I could not hear a thing. My motionless crippled body, now a bag of bones, lie awkwardly contorted in the snow facing the sky, next to the buck I had slayed scarcely a moment ago. Talk about cruel and bitter irony. Rather, maybe there was divine purpose at work. There was no way to know which. Either way, I was in serious trouble. I could not understand how this happened. What had I done wrong? My lungs, like popped damaged balloons, refused to inflate. My blood spilled from my chest, spoiling the snow. I could only watch as it snaked its way toward the slain buck beside me. But for my eyes, I was paralyzed. I turned my gaze toward the dark clouds blanketing the frozen earth. A moment later my son appeared over me, blocking my view of the comforting fluffy snow-filled clouds above. He stood tall over me with a panicked look on his face.

It was like watching a silent movie. His mouth moved without sound. He had to be saying something, but whatever it was, I could not discern it above the buzzing in my ears. I was trying to breathe, but I couldn't capture a single breath. I would not be allowed to borrow anymore air. Of the many lessons I would learn, this was the first. In that moment, I learned that it's all borrowed. As I lay there, I thought about that. How the air we breathe is merely borrowed. All of life is borrowed. All of the things we acquire, our experiences, family, friends, even our memories, the food we eat, water we drink. We believe we own these things. But the reality is they are all borrowed. This revelation summed up all of life. A complex series of loans and borrowings. Then, either through intention, age, or accident, all we love and cherish, along with all we abhor, are all taken from us and returned, scattered to the ends of the world.

I had the misfortune of experiencing a similar sensation when I was eight years old. Four of the toughest kids in the neighborhood came walking down our street looking for trouble. Eddie Cavallero led their pack. As tough as he was, everyone in the know, knew to not tussle with Eddie because his three older brothers were known for cracking the skulls of anyone who messed with their family. Eddie spotted us and challenged us to a dodgeball game. We never backed away from a challenge. They threw down the gauntlet. We accepted. Big mistake. It was then I got schooled on the consequences that come from getting hit in the chest with that distinct red rubber dodgeball when thrown by a boy three times my size. I tried to catch the ball, instead it caught me. The impact was an explosion that drove out all of the air from my lungs, making it impossible to catch my breath. I thought I was going to die. I literally saw stars and bright lights flashing and twinkling around the corners of my eyes. I chased after my breath, but it took minutes before I could breathe again. Eddie and his crew laughed the entire time. That, I had always remembered, was something I did not want to experience again.

Now, on a cold mountain, with my chest exposed, my lungs deflated and my blood emptying out of me, there was no recovery. It was moving fast, leaving all breath behind. It was then I understood I was going to die. Anger surged, transported by the adrenaline already coursing through me. I assumed it was my son who shot me since he was the first to reach me and so quickly after I had been hit. I wanted to scream, *Are you a moron*? But quickly, a wave of nausea hit and my heart broke. I may have grown a little angry over the years, but I loved my family, even if I did not always express it. I understood this moment would burden him for the rest of his life. He knelt over me, his face was red. Tears and sweat dripped from him onto me. I wanted to tell him that it was ok. I wanted to tell him, *Sorry*. I wanted to tell him I loved him. Something I had not said to him in years. Even if I could, I am not sure I would have had the courage. But, I could not say any of those things. My thoughts became hazy and I had difficulty concentrating. An odd, unsettled peace, began to seize me. The buzz in my ears faded. I was like the sea at low tide, calmly ebbing in and out. I forced myself to think of my family and my children. If this was death, I would not be there for them. Profound sadness washed over me laying siege to the calm and peacefulness that began to take control. I wanted to sleep and run from it. I tried to fight and stay awake. I tried to hold on. There was nothing left for me to do. My gaze moved from my son to the heavens above. I had been baptized as a baby. I went to church semi-regularly. I was hopeful I would be okay, but I admit, doubt and dread lingered. My life wasn't supposed to end like this. I wasn't supposed to die like an animal on a frozen mountain. It wasn't my time. I became too weak to fight. A last shiver, then numb, then . . . dark.

B. Lee Baker

The Second Chapter

Despite my Catholic upbringing, secretly, I always questioned what came next and feared deep down that there was nothing. No heaven. No hell. Nothing. Just the abyss. That all-encompassing darkness with no light, no sound, and no thought; created by the universe or God to do one thing, consume and extinguish my soul. As stupid as this may sound, I always preferred the thought of eternal suffering over nothing. You can really tie your mind in a knot thinking about the idea of nothing. If there was nothing, I wouldn't be, so there would be nothing to experience. Nothing to feel. Nothing to miss. So why concern myself. Or, would I experience the monster of nothingness as it feasted and digested my spirit? But it wasn't really that either that bothered me so much; the process of being eliminated. I assumed death would do that job. Rather, what truly haunted my thoughts, was that I would simply no longer be and yet somehow know it. Not being able to witness or know about those things which I cared about most. That was it, being cutoff; that was my greatest fear.

A sudden violent jolt answered part of my lifelong question. I was being pulled. Actually, more accurately, sucked, out of my body. The feeling was like holding onto a cliff with the unrelenting force of gravity pulling at you. Only this sensation was jerking me upwards. The force felt similar to when a dental surgeon pulls, tugs, and then finally extracts a bottom molar. The stubborn rooted tooth holding on, refusing to let go of its home. I swear I heard a pop when I was finally freed from my body. I instantly sped upward. The movement was comparable to riding a behemoth rollercoaster heading in reverse. I felt like a rope was tied around my waist and pulling me through a tunnel traveling backwards. It was fast and I felt the force of being ripped from this world, whipped around like a rag doll travelling up into the sky. The air slapped at my ears, the sensation similar to sticking your head out of the window of a moving car. I estimated only moments had passed between slipping into unconsciousness and my separation from this world, but I understood that, at least for a brief time, I had fallen into that darkness that I so much feared. It was only upon the return to consciousness that I understood

I had been in the nothing. I shivered knowing I didn't want to go back. I was grateful to be out. At first, I wasn't absolutely certain I was dead. I was moving fast, but I knew something was wrong. Rather than turn forward to see where I was going, I turned back and caught sight of my bloody, broken, body sunk in the snow. My heartbeat accelerated. What had once been my body, was now a useless vessel of damaged meat, dressed in camouflage green. I knew then, I was dead. It was my due date. I guess Sandy, the bitch, got the last laugh.

The scene was grisly. The surrounding white snow now stained crimson from my blood and the entrails of the dead buck. My former eyes were open and held a dead stare directly at me as I travelled upward. I could see the crater in my chest and my son crouching over me. It was mere moments ago I had crouched over the dead buck in a similar manner. Irony sometimes reveals itself in twisted ways. I tried to move back toward myself. I called to my son. I shouted above the whipping wind,

"Nooooo!"

He did not hear me.

I was so focused on the sack of flesh that was once me, I didn't notice the buck, just ahead, also travelling up into the heavens above. However, down below, the beast's earthly body remained next to mine on the cold ground. I blinked excessively trying to discern what I was seeing. In light of what happened, I was certain the animal would probably remain on that spot to rot. Such a shame. I was going to mount its head in my office. Now, the worms, insects and other beasts of the mountain would feast on it, leaving no record it was ever alive. Yet, inexplicably, the now ethereal animal and I flew together toward some unknown destination. As we began to move faster, I turned to the buck and we locked eyes. The buck then smiled perversely at me. The awkward grin stirred a feeling of deep dread and I became alarmed that I would return to my maker alone and empty handed with my last memory of a buck's mocking smile. The indifferent, indiscriminate, maker of death waited with open arms, ready to accept the cruel and brutal delivery of another unwilling victim. The journey ended with a collision with something I did not see. The dreaded darkness returned.

This time, in place of nothingness, in the depths of the blackness, I moved through space and time in the blink of an eye. I saw snippets of what I believed to be events back home. I could not know for sure if it was a dream or reality. I saw my body being transported back near my home in New Jersey. I was given a Catholic funeral. Which is to say my family followed the ritual dictated by the church. I had always been comforted by knowing what to do, and when, especially in the midst of a crisis. Having a ritual to follow made it easier, to cruise on autopilot, and not have to think about what had really happened. Not really. Follow the ritual; get through it; move on.

The funeral home, like most, was a house of death. It served no other purpose. An assembly line of precision designed to move the dead into the back, and then out through the front. A final trip on the way to the church before going in the ground. Everything about the place spoke death. Even the clashing decomposing carpet and curtains were morbid. If they could talk, what would these things expose about the thousands of mourners every year treading and trampling around? What would the private hushed side conversations reveal about the dead? Better yet, what would they expose about those who lived on? The place smelled like death. The signature stench of formaldehyde and embalming fluid floated above the scents of the flowers, candles, perfume and cologne that bathed my mourners. The place could never be used for any other purpose. It would have to be put to death itself, knocked down, and buried before it could be used for anything else.

My wake in this house of death was gruesome. I watched in horror as my love and best friend, my wife, Grace, sat stoically like a drugged zombie. The shock and despair mixed with valium made her semi-catatonic. I felt her suffering. I wanted to hold her. I wanted to be with my family. Maybe this is hell. Watching the anguish, unable to do anything about it. My body was brought in the back well before the ceremony began. The crowd gathered in the front and I could see a lengthy receiving line that extended out the door and into the parking lot. However, most who attended were professional colleagues who felt obligated to show. Lawyers. Enough said. No one wanted to be the odd man out. Many of them quietly complained.

"There was not enough parking," but quickly added, "what a nice turnout."

That was supposed to make the family, or those who really cared, feel better. A nice turnout. I watched most of them frequently, and with failed subtlety, look at their phones and watches. They wondered to themselves how long, was just long enough, before they could get out of there. They wore suits. Made it easy for them to pay their respects right after work. They showed up. Followed the ritual. They did their duty and went to bed knowing they were "good people." The truth was that most who showed didn't really care.

Not really. They may have said to one another that my death was sad. They may have even felt bad for my son, given the circumstances. But those sentiments were momentary. Fleeting. My passing wouldn't leave any lasting scar or unfillable void. They were just thankful it wasn't them.

My picture sat atop my polished silver coffin, adorned with fancy silver hardware. More photos on a cheap stand, provided by the funeral home, were displayed next to it. Many of them were me in my hunting attire posed, pridefully, along with the various carnage I caused. Me and my selfie stick. Holding my rifle. I had to look away. Seeing these photos from this vantage stirred something within me that just didn't sit well.

Why did they choose those pictures? I wondered. I didn't like it. It was a closed casket. I guess I didn't look so hot after what I had been through. Watching, I experienced nothing but sadness. Sadness I was no longer there. Sadness I could not comfort my family and tell them everything would be ok. Even if I could, I didn't know for sure if it would be. I watched as my despondent, inconsolable son sat alone. I wanted to weep for him. My heart broke for him the most. I wanted to weep for the life I lost. I wanted to tell many of my mourners to go home. To stay away. I was allowed none of it.

It took them longer than usual to dig my grave. The faded green frozen earth, covered in white permafrost, was unforgiving. The deep freeze in the northeast at the time of my death had come early this year and had not let up at the time of my burial. At my gravesite everyone was dressed in black. I watched the frigid air consume the warm breath escaping the mouths of my mourners. I wanted to tell them that it was all borrowed. They shivered and struggled to stay warm. They were too cold to cry. But, with good effort and determination, I was placed in the ground. And, just like that, Lou Pastore, aka, the Animal Killer, was done.

The Third Chapter

I woke up to a dream.

Neither alive, nor dead. Not in heaven, not in hell; I was instead inside a pliable sac filled with pink fluid. I held my breath for fear of swallowing the foreign substance and suffocating. My heart pounded violently. I couldn't see a thing beyond the membrane wall. I extended my arm, making a fist, and tried to penetrate the enclosure, but it stretched and held. I was sickened. I sensed the sac was careening through space. I closed my eyes tightly and tensed every muscle in my body in anticipation of a violent impact that could come at any moment. It felt like being blindfolded on an inflated tube, then projected into the air at the world's tallest, most intense, waterpark. My stomach churned. Without warning, I hit the ground with a hard slap, exploding the bubble holding me. The fluid scattered, then quickly evaporated. I gasped for air as my chest heaved. I found myself lying on the floor of a warm flat surface. Opening my eyes, I was still unable to see a thing. The darkness was so complete, and devoid of any light, that when I moved my hand before my face, I couldn't see it. I wondered if I had gone blind from the fall. I slowly stood, but my disorientation thickened. An overpowering smell, similar to antiseptic and rubbing alcohol, consumed me, making me gag. I bent over and retched. At first nothing came up. I felt so sick, that had I not already been dead, I would have begged for death to come. Finally, I gratefully expelled the pink fluid sloshing in my belly. When the nausea passed, I tried to compose myself.

Turning, I saw a faint light far-off the horizon penetrating the luxurious darkness. As I stared, the light grew and advanced toward me in an unnatural way. Rather than being a fixed point in the distance, I watched the light travel to me. It called to me. Behind me, a cool breeze coming from the dark carried creepy, indiscernible, sounds, summoning me to come. A chill ran down my spine into my groin causing me to clench my teeth. I thought I heard a cry for help echoing from its depths. Between moving toward the cold crying dark or the calling light, the brilliant glow appeared to be the better of my two options; the only apparent way out of the uncomfortable darkness. I needed fresh air. My sickness was returning from the sterile smell pervading this dismal chamber. The stench reminded me of a hospital. That fake clean that merely masked the filth and disease that lies beneath the surface. The smell offering false comfort, designed to delude its visitors into believing that hospitals are place to go to get well, when they are really places to go to die. A reminder that not all things are as they appear. I sheepishly walked to meet the light, assuming and hoping its origin was an exit. As the light increased, I began to make out my surroundings. The walls and floor were marble like and shinned with perfection. The walls stretched up, beyond my sight. I looked upward, but due to the darkness or its height, or both, I couldn't see the ceiling. As I moved, my surroundings became brighter and more in focus. I looked up in amazement. It was like being inside a hollow skyscraper.

Still dressed in my hunting fatigues and boots, they were cumbersome and becoming stiff and gamy from being inside the wet sac. Without warning, the memories of my death came screaming back, erupting and forcing their unwanted reality upon me. I instinctively clutched at my chest and tried to suck in as much air as possible. Mercifully, my body was intact. But, I wasn't quite the same. I was not exactly weightless, but I was very light on my feet. I felt like I could hop several yards with an effortless leap, like astronauts walking on the moon. With no other visible option, I continued to move forward. As I proceeded, I suddenly saw something in the darkness move ahead of me. It also moved toward the light. But the darkness continued to consume the light making it difficult to confirm what I thought I was seeing. For some inexplicable reason, the image of the smiling buck leaped into my mind. And, as it became brighter, I saw that the outline of an animal that resembled a deer. *Was that what moved just ahead of me? The deer I had conquered just before I was shot?* I slowed my thoughts. *Why would it be here?* I tried to quicken my pace, but could not catch whatever outpaced me ahead. The only sound in the place was a constant soothing hum from some unknown source and the rhythmic gallop of the thing several yards in front of me.

I finally reached the exit of the chamber without having caught whatever it was ahead of me. The light, now stuck at the threshold of the tunnel, was so bright, it acted as an opaque curtain hiding what lay beyond the firmament separating the other side. I would be required to take a leap of faith through. I unconsciously held my breath and stepped out of the tube.

It took more than a moment for my eyes to adjust. When they did, my brain twisted. It couldn't process the scene before me. It was unlike anything I had ever seen or imagined. I was at the bottom of a canyon. In the distance, a giant staircase sprouted from the ground and stretched up to the entrance of a bone white colossal coliseum structure. More accurately, it was part coliseum, part cathedral, part temple that sat atop a mountain. The structure's texture was so clean and smooth it glistened. It was so brilliant, it was difficult to stare at directly. It reminded me of a program I had watched on television that opined that when the great pyramids of Giza were first built they were so smooth they sparkled and reflected the sun. The grand structure before me was a marriage of architecture, blending the *Parthenon* and the *Coliseum* in Rome. However, the size defied all understanding. The staircase itself seemed to rise hundreds of feet and stretched on for miles, as it completely encircled and wrapped the structure. I thought reaching the top would be an impossible feat, akin to climbing a mountain. Gigantic did not sufficiently describe the size of the structure itself. The Grand Canyon came to mind, but this dwarfed that. I imagined my father asking, *Who the hell paid to build that thing*? I laughed to myself and a pang of deep loss hit me. I missed my dad. I wanted to go home. I wanted to see my family. I wanted my life back. The life stolen and cut short. I wanted to speak to my son and hold my wife. Still, I wondered what waited for me inside. No matter, I could not escape the invisible force that pulled me toward the structure.

Thousands of these tubes, identical to the one I exited, punctured and surrounded the canyon walls. Each one only a few feet apart from one another. Each, looked like a tunnel that had been burrowed into the side of a mountain. Long, smooth, and white identical walkways led the way from each of these tubes to the staircase. In between the walkways grew flawless green grass that was so perfect it resembled carpet. There was nowhere to go, but toward the stairs. Then, as if I suddenly woke from a dream, I realized I was not alone. Far from it. My attention became fixated on the animal that emerged from the chamber just ahead of me. I called out to it.

"Hey!" I shouted.

I could feel several pairs of eyes turn to me, but I remained focused on the deer ahead. It walked with an odd limp. I wanted to confirm he was the deer I had killed just before I had been shot. I was almost certain it was.

I tried again. "Hey, you."

Not breaking its stride, the deer turned its head back to shoot me a glance, and grinned. The same smirk he had offered on the ride to this place. An image I will not soon forget, the smirking dead deer sailing through the clouds.

"Hey! I'm talking to you. Why do you keep smirking at me? And what's so funny?"

He ignored me, and continued on with his hitched gallop. No matter how hard I tried, I could not catch him. The constant melody of a faint breeze and the sound of the broken stride of the mass of souls I had yet to fully observe was all I heard.

I abandoned my effort to reach the animal, gathered myself, and garnered the courage to turn away from the wondrous structure ahead to survey the other beings filling the valley. The scene utterly confounded me. In death, shock and disbelief was quickly becoming my new norm. I was forced to suspend all I had come to understand. Millions of other souls joined me on this pilgrimage to the unknown. Not limited to humans, they consisted of cats, dogs, insects, birds and every creature known. Every kind of fish from the ocean, every little and large thing that crawled, walked, ran and swung on the Earth; every kind of bird that flew in the skies above.

Nothing came out from the structure atop the mountain. A few tried to return into the tunnels from where they came, but an invisible force stopped them and swiftly sent them toward the stairs. We were all submerged in the canyon, souls flooding every inch of available space, like cold water filling a swimming pool. It overflowed with sojourners, so much so, that I feared we would soon be clogged and buried if we were not quickly emptied. There was nowhere else to go but up. But for a few exceptions, no one, no thing, said a word or made a sound. Those that did, quietly whimpered. Pulled by the same mystical and unseen force, we all headed in the same direction toward the temple above and our fate that awaited us inside.

While it was similar to the Earth, the air in this place was a little different. A little too perfect. It was sweet and the sky was more purple than blue. It was majestic, with just the right number of puffy white clouds painted on it. It was so perfect, it appeared almost fake. We all continued to move forward, no one gaining on the other and no one falling behind. It seemed I no longer had a say in what I could or could not do. Death destroyed my free will.

I began to ascend the steps. I say ascend because it wouldn't be accurate to describe it as a climb. It was too easy. Gravity did not have the same force here that it did back on Earth. Had it been a climb, it would have required much more effort and taken much more time. Time also ticked differently.

Animal Killer

Even though my ascent was somewhat effortless, time became elastic and stretched contorting my understanding of just how to mark its passage. My ascension may have taken minutes or days, I could not be sure. I felt I died only moments ago, and yet, I had watched my funeral and now was in this place. The lack of time perception was more disruptive and disorienting than anything else.

Halfway up, I gained an improved view of the structure. An engraving in the stone on the front of the triangular facade that sat atop the pillars guarding the entry read, "Qui reddet unicuique secundum opera eius." I had no idea what that meant. So much for the Latin classes I was forced to attend at Saint Mary's in Brooklyn. Back then, I would have received a hearty *whack* across the knuckles with a wooden ruler, followed by the *woosh* of a smack to the head for not knowing the meaning. My father enthusiastically granted the nuns specific permission to "give it to me" if I misbehaved and had it coming. And, I often had it coming.

I continued upward. As I neared the top, I wondered if the entrance was the mythical pearly gates. *Would I meet Saint Peter? Would I be allowed in?* No one seemed to be turned away. Truth be told, now that I was out of the darkness of the abyss, I was no longer concerned what would happen next. I reminded myself that I believed in Jesus. As a Catholic, that meant I was covered. Nothing else mattered. It was all the others here that needed to be concerned. The nonbelievers and the animals. They were the ones who should be worried what would happen next and where they were headed. My worry and fear gradually melted away. I became even a little excited and anxious to see what lay before me. The horror connected to the circumstances resulting in my death began to fade. With each step, the insignificant trifling memories of life dissolved. I fought the brain fog that began to smother me. How much time had passed? I didn't think anything could make me forget my family. But with each step, the excitement to enter what so clearly had to be heaven, overtook me. Sadness and loss left me. What would await me inside? A swell of questions swirled. Would I speak with God and learn all the whys of the world and all the secrets of the heavens?

I advanced toward the entrance of the temple. The same unseen force that pulled each being up the stairs and to the opening of the structure also funneled each into a single line just before the doorway. I fought the smothering haze and battled to remain oriented. Moving forward, I staggered with each step. It was the same feeling as losing your sea legs. A flash from my honeymoon reminded me how I felt after a seven day Bermuda cruise. When it was over and I was back on firm land, I still felt the sway to and fro, as if I were at sea. Missing here was the distinct salty scent of the ocean air which I loved so much. I looked back over my shoulder and scanned the valley below. I surveyed the landscape and watched thousands of souls continuously emerging from the tubes, all heading toward the stairs. I could not believe how far I had come. Hours must have passed, but I was unsure. I should have been exhausted, but felt fine. Closer to the top of the stairs, I was able to view the enormous entrance. Two bronze doors two hundred feet tall stood open. A replica of the tablets containing the Ten Commandments were inscribed upon each door. Below each tablet, engraved into the doors, were the words of the Bible, Genesis to Revelation. Old Testament on the left door. New Testament on the right. I wondered if these doors ever closed and what it would mean if they did. One at a time, we entered.

The grinning deer just before me.

Finally, at the top, I stepped through and entered into a vast round hall only moments after the deer, but it was gone. I looked around and wondered where it disappeared. My fixation on the deer vanished though when I scanned and registered the depth and breadth of the cavernous hall. The dome that lie atop this rotunda was open in the center allowing the light to flood spectacularly inside. I staggered back, my mouth agape, when I noticed the moving mural that adorned the ceiling and walls. At first, I thought it was simply a painted fresco, but it was actually a motion picture of moving paint. I wondered how this was possible. It was a painting, but it moved like a movie.

I stared in amazement as I watched the biography of the world unfold. It started amidst flawless darkness. Then, the perfect powerful hand of God tore through a pin-sized circle of white light that expanded as His hand up to His elbow emerged. God snapped his fingers causing an explosion of creation of cosmic materials. They bloomed and collided together, cooling and then settling to form the outline of the Earth and stars in the sky. It reminded me of Michelangelo's *Creation of Adam* which decorates the ceiling of the Sistine Chapel. Only this was far more magnificent and God's face remained hidden.

God's voice then boomed and reverberated throughout the rotunda with the unmistakable first command, "Let there be light!" There was a flash and I was momentarily blinded. I then watched and listened to the events of the next six days unfold. I watched how God created the world we know. I witnessed the creation of Adam and Eve and their fall from grace. I watched the flood and Noah, Moses leading the Jews out of Egypt and into the dessert. I did not, would not, blink, as I watched and listened to Jesus Christ in a meadow looking up to his unseen father, volunteering to come to Earth to be a sacrifice for the condemned masses. I then saw his birth, crucifixion and resurrection. All of this told in moving, painted pictures. I was overjoyed. My mood, since my death, which had been swinging like a pendulum, moving from dread to hope, now firmly fixated on hope.

What lifelong doubts I carried with me vanished right there. I could not help but wonder what non-believers thought when they stepped into this place and watched and heard what I just heard and witnessed. Maybe they were shown a different story. If not, it had to be a punch to the gut. Reality hits hardest when you're not ready for it. They say there are few atheists in fox holes. I suspect there were none in this place. Funny thing about what we believe to be true, it sometimes has very little relationship to what actually is. And, when our mind is finally confronted with the undisputable concrete evidence of truth, our former belief shames us and we realize our misguided passionate conviction of what we thought was true, really meant nothing.

When the movie ended, I looked around and noticed there were hundreds of dark wooden arched doors every few feet that encircled the rotunda. Each was not quite as large as the entry to the hall, but were enormous themselves. They were all closed, with no handles or locks. The sounds coming from the other side of these doors were both comforting and terrifying. Behind some, I could hear crowds cheer. Behind others, I heard the sounds of war and cries for help. Some blared the sounds of blissful music. Some contained sounds of joy, laughter and comfort. The smells from each blended in the hall, forming a mixture of sweetness that reminded me of the fragrant aroma of Bermuda air, spoiled by the unmistakable odor of burning flesh and death. Which door was for me I pondered?

The Fourth Chapter

From the corner of my eye I saw something move. I turned to see an ancient, well-built man, dressed in a brilliant white robe approaching me. I hadn't noticed him when I first entered the hall, and didn't see where he came from. He had been observing me watch the living fresco; evaluating my reaction. The two of us alone occupied the cavernous rotunda. No one had entered after me. Time seemed to stand still. As he moved closer, I observed that he was freakishly tall with an impressive physique, gladiator-like. Guessing, I'd measure him at least eight feet tall. His straight, jet black, hair was slicked-backed. His hands were oddly thick. Only his eyes betrayed his age and revealed he was a man who'd seen a billion deaths; yet, there was no sadness in them. Instead, they signaled indifference. Everything about him exuded indifference. Despite that, he was a physical marvel and no sane man would want to find out what it took to move him from indifference to rage.

Still smiling from my excitement and the amazement of this place, I called out to him as he approached, "That was really something," I said, pointing to the fresco. "What happened to that deer that came in before me?"

My voice echoed and reverberated throughout the hall. He said nothing as he continued to glide toward me. When he was upon me, only inches away, the giant leaned down so we were nose to nose, and then he spoke.

"Please follow me. No doubt you have questions." He turned and guided me toward one of the wooden doors and continued, "Before you ask, yes, Louie. You're dead. So that answers that." He said with little compassion. "This is what you wanted to know, yes?"

He confirmed what I already knew. But still, I had doubts, given I had never been dead before. I hoped somehow I was wrong and that all of this was just a bad dream or some near death experience. I thought maybe I would open my eyes in a hospital with my family surrounding me.

"That's not what I asked."

He ignored my snarky response, "Now the hard part begins. We have some difficult work ahead of us," he said as his eyes looked elsewhere.

He allowed his words to linger. He sounded like a man with a job to do. My pulse quickened and he turned to me. I wondered if he could hear my heart thump inside my chest. My smile fled and my mood soured. I wondered what that meant . . . *now the hard part begins*.

He stopped at one of the colossal arched doors and tapped it.

"This way." He directed.

The arched doorway opened to a tall, narrow tunnel. He stepped inside and I followed.

"What do you mean, now the hard part begins?" I asked.

"Answers will come."

The door immediately shut behind me. He was so tall he could barely fit. His head almost hit the ceiling. The passageway was lined with dark, damp, brick. A distinct, long forgotten, smell hit me reminding me of the sleeping gas my dentist used to knock me out so he could rip two teeth from my mouth when I was fourteen years old. The odor made me nauseous and fouled my declining mood. We came upon a slight incline to the tunnel, but I kept pace with the giant leading me.

"What happened to the deer?" My voice echoed in the confined space.

That provoked him to slow his march forward, pausing for a moment. He turned to me and he raised his voice repeating my question, "What happened to the deer? Why do you ask? Do you care?"

There was no hostility or sarcasm to his tone. He wanted to know, like the answer was somehow critically important to some decision.

"I don't care. I just want to know what this place is and why it's here with me. I just killed it." I hadn't lost my prideful smug tone.

He exhaled letting out an *"Hmpf,"* turned, and resumed his stride up the tunnel.

With his back to me he offered, "What will happen to the deer will be justice."

"Next question. What is this place? Purgatory?"

"No, not purgatory."

We continued up the tunnel. Getting information from this guy was like pulling teeth, it was very frustrating.

"I am not going anywhere until I get some answers!" I broke stride and folded my arms in defiance.

Ignoring my tantrum, he said, "You should prepare yourself, Louie. Where you are, and what happens now, you should know, is just. It must be. There is no other way. It is what it is. And you are what you are. Resisting will only make things worse."

Animal Killer

Unsatisfied, I wanted to stop following him, but an irresistible force, and curiosity, drove me forward. As we neared the end of the tunnel, I could hear the swell of a crowd unlike any I had ever heard. It was similar to the sound that hit you when entering a baseball stadium, growing and building in intensity as you stepped out from the concession areas and into the stadium itself. The tunnel opened onto the floor of a gigantic oval outdoor coliseum, revealing a spectacular scene. The floor's width and length extended for miles. The interior of the structure matched the outside of the temple I had entered. The stone, so white and smooth, it glowed. The waiting crowd exploded the moment we stepped out from the tunnel. The sound nearly knocked me off my feet. It was so deafening and debilitating that it made the fantastic scene that much more difficult to process. Still staggering, the equally powerful odor of an unkempt zoo followed the assault to my senses. A mixture of peanuts, rotting food and animals. I spun around taking it all in. The extent and span of the arena defied logic. Then there was the crowd. A bewilderment beyond imagination. The screaming spectators were made up of thousands, maybe more accurately, millions, of every form of life that had ever inhabited the Earth. The sight was breathtaking and simultaneously terrifying.

Everything from dinosaurs to dogs. Giraffes to zebras. Squirrels to bison, and everything in between. Missing, were the humans, I couldn't locate a single man or woman. A massive metal fence surrounded the base and rose from the floor of the arena holding them back. Many slammed their bodies and limbs against it causing it to sway and bend. Monkeys clung to the fence shaking it, trying to tear it down. My heart raced as I feared it would topple and I would be overrun and attacked. They all shouted and hissed and roared. Amazingly, the predator-prey relationships so natural on Earth in the animal kingdom did not exist in this crowd. They were unified, singularly focused on me.

I followed my guide as he walked to the center of the arena floor where an elevated platform lay. The setting reminded me of the Mohmand Ali versus George Foreman fight in Zaire, Africa. The pugilistic ring had been erected in the middle of an enormous outdoor arena. When Ali entered and made his way inside the ropes, welcoming and encouraging cheers greeted him. The unfortunate Foreman entered as a pariah to jeers and hisses. The role of villain thrust upon him. I felt like Foreman and recalled that things did not end well for him. Frightened about my fate, I wondered what came next and hoped things would end better for me.

Animal Killer

As we made our way, I screamed over the multitude, "How is this possible? What are they shouting?"

He didn't respond. He didn't flinch, unsure if he heard me. The thunder of the unintelligible congregation did not relent as we walked. When we reached the platform, without hesitation, he moved up a stone staircase. The platform was also carved from stone. I reached the top and was struck by the familiar design. The few pieces of furniture were arranged similar to a world court tribunal. A stone bench surrounded by a square wooden rail was on the left and an identical enclosed bench that faced it was on the right. They were separated by some distance. In between them, and set back, sat ten stone chairs with high back rests arranged in a semicircle facing these two enclosed lone benches. Off to the far left was a giant bronze statue of a man. The figure stood fifty feet tall. Affixed on the base was an inscription that read, "King Solomon– All Israel heard of the judgment which the king had judged; and they feared the king: for they saw that the wisdom of God was in him, to do judgment." The statue was magnificent. His chiseled face, strong, confident and bearded. A king's crown sat atop his head. A fitting tribute for the man known for wisdom and fairness who'd been anointed by God Himself. Solomon held an old fashioned working double pan balance scale made of silver. The familiar scale held by Lady Justice in many courthouses where I had made my living. The two weighing pans of the scale, held by chains, lay suspended only feet from the ground.

"There." He pointed to the bench on the left, "That's where you sit when we begin."

As I absorbed and adjusted to the sights and sounds, I began to regain my composure. I still had so many questions, but with the deafening noise it was difficult to hear myself think.

Reading my mind again, he offered, "Here it will be decided whether you go back, move on, or be banished to Oblivion."

I shouted to him again over the rising roar from the throngs of shouting creatures who continued to violently rock the fence back and forth.

"Go back? Go back, where?"

"Back to Earth."

"Why would I go back? How could I go back?"

"All things are possible with God."

"And, what do you mean, banished to Oblivion? What is this place?"

"Did you read the engraving embedded atop the entrance of this place when you entered?"

"I want answers!" I shouted.

Unfazed, he continued, "The engraving. *Qui reddet unicuique secundum opera eius.* It is Latin. It means, He will render to each one according to his works."

My face twisted.

"You're surprised," he mocked. "How can this be? I am quite sure you know exactly what that means. After all, you were a good Catholic. Isn't that so? This cannot come as a surprise to you. Upon your transition from the life God gave you, He renders upon you what you have earned."

Memories of a fiery priest who presided over our church for a short time sprung back to me. Without fail, he ended every mass with the same quote from the book of Romans, '*you are storing up wrath against yourself for the day of wrath, when God's righteous judgment will be revealed. God will repay each one according to his deeds. To those who by perseverance in doing good seek glory, honor, and immortality, He will give eternal life. But for those who are self-seeking and who reject the truth and follow wickedness, there will be wrath and anger.*' I had never really given these words much thought. I dismissed such sentiments thinking it was the church's attempt to scare, manipulate and control its followers. I never considered the very real consequences that might flow from them.

Sensing my understanding, he continued, "I am the embodiment of this principal. I am Karma. I am one of the twelve. I make certain you reap what you sow."

Karma paused.

Reap what I sow? That sounded like a threat. I began to think it was time to worry.

"Karma?" I asked confused.

"That's right."

I stared and blinked reflexively, trying to process what he said.

"What do you mean reap what I sow?"

"Come on, Louie, what exactly did you think happened when you passed? Did you honestly believe there was an open invitation into the Kingdom? That there would be no judgment? No consequences for your sin?"

"I . . . uh . . . I– guess I didn't. But, Karma?"

"Why is that so hard to believe? Many have called my name. Few have fully understood its meaning. Quite simply, I work the will of God and make sure you get exactly what you deserve."

"Get exactly what I deserve? But I was–"

"A good Catholic. I know." He interrupted. "But there is more to it than that, Louie. The Kingdom of Heaven is perfection. All are invited, but narrow is the path that leads to the gate of heaven. Walk the narrow path, follow the word of God, live a life of righteousness and be welcomed. Stray from the path, and perish. Remember, the

Bible cautions, 'Not everyone who says to me, Lord, Lord, will enter into the kingdom of heaven – only the one who does the will of my Father in heaven.' You know this. Only those beings who embody perfection are welcomed. God will not allow less than perfection of spirit into the Kingdom of Heaven. The purpose of life is to shed yourself of the evils of the world so that you may enter. I have worked very hard to make sure you had every opportunity to do right. To repent and renew. To shed yourself of the evil you have done, and which has been done to you. To return you to the path when you strayed. I nudged and pushed, and now you find yourself here. I do not judge, I merely observe and provide the opportunity for you to give and get justice so that you may move on. In this place, there is no right or wrong, only what is because of what was."

"So this is not Purgatory and it's not Heaven?"

"No Louie, this is not the Kingdom of Heaven. The Kingdom of Heaven is far more magnificent. More grand. Indescribable. This is the place God metes out karma and judgment. Where He renders according to your deeds. Did you do good deeds, Louie?"

I looked down and considered his question, not responding immediately.

Before I could, he continued, "If it is determined that you lack perfection of spirit, if we believe there is no hope for you, if you are unable to become the being you were meant to be, you will be sent to the *Spiritus Exterminatore*, the Spirit Destroyer."

"Well that sounds pretty fucking awful. What the hell is the Spirit Destroyer?" I asked angrily. "So, only perfect people enter Heaven? That sounds fair. Must be a pretty empty place." I said smugly.

"No need to be perverse. You should take caution. You are in a holy place. Close to God. You should show more respect. But of course, how you behave is your decision and within your control alone. It has always been so and it is what has led you to this moment. If you are lost, you will go to the Spirit Destroyer who will perform his duty. He will feast upon your soul and leave you banished to Oblivion. Your spirit will be destroyed and you will be no more. You will not know God, nor receive His grace. Your soul will be annihilated and you will be no more."

To embellish the point, he opened his fist to reveal several grains of sand. With a short, quick burst, he blew across his palm. The sand scattered and disappeared before hitting the ground. He continued.

Animal Killer

"This is not what God wants for you, but at some point, you must understand, even though the Lord loves you, He must let go if you are truly lost. He will mourn you, but He will not allow anyone or anything to spoil the Kingdom. And, no, Louie, not only perfect people enter, I said perfect in spirit. Someone who desires to please the Lord. Someone who accepts His will. To allow anything less than that would debase the beauty of the Kingdom. There's no need to be angry, Louie, you should simply focus on what is, and what should be, and know, the Lord wants you, and expects you, to become the being you were meant to be. But, it has always been up to you. And, as I know you like to say, therein lies the rub. Did you live well? Did you follow His word? His desires? Or did you become ensnared by the trappings of the material world? Did you love your neighbor as you loved yourself? These are the questions that must be answered, before you move on."

How about a little compassion, I just died for Christ's sake! I thought to myself and almost said aloud. My body tensed. Karma's to the point, unemotional, blunt message angered me. Worse, his description of the delivery of my soul for destruction and illustration of the scattering sand terrified me.

"Do I get to know what it is that I did or didn't do that fails to satisfy your standard of perfection?"

I curtly asked, glaring at him, demanding an answer.

"You assume you fall short? *Hmmm*, telling. It hasn't yet been decided, but yes, Louie, you will get to know. Remember, you alone choose the being you are to be, and where you finish. This has always been so. One thing that never changes is that God loves you, He wants you with Him. If He didn't, you would already be no more. Whatever is decided and what you experience in this place is meant to fulfill what karma and justice demand for your deeds."

"God loves me?" I motioned to the screaming crowd. "This does not look like love. This does not sound like love. Why are all these animals here? How are they shouting? Why are they so angry?"

"They are angry because you, and people just like you, have hunted them and slain them without pause or pity. You didn't respect them or appreciate their sacrifices. They are afraid of you, Louie. They fear the Animal Killer. They fear you will be allowed in and permitted to desecrate the Kingdom, the same way evil had been invited in to spoil Eden. They fear having to dwell there with you. To live in paradise with a man who persecuted them for sport and hated them is no paradise at all. So, in this place, they get their say."

With that, and with no microphone or speaker system, he looked up into the crowd and spoke. His voice boomed like thunder and he bellowed, "The Lord does not make mistakes, and neither do we who work His will."

His statement was so loud it carried for miles, to the corners of the arena. Every being present heard him. His words seemed to simultaneously satiate and stir the mob, instigating even louder cries, feeding their anger.

"So– that's what this is about?" I interrupted. "The deer I shot? I can explain! I don't belong here. Send me back please. You said that was an option. I can explain things to you, then you can return me back to my life."

He shot me a scolding glance with a stern reprimand,

"Now is not the time for that, Louie."

"Now is not the time? If not now, when is the time? I want a chance to explain!"

"No." He said dismissively.

"Fine!"

I felt like I was about to get railroaded. I didn't know the rules, this place or the players. I had been a lawyer long enough to see what happens in these circumstances. Once you get caught up in the system, it's never a fair fight. Despite the tough facade I put forth, fundamentally, I was frightened and panicked to the core. It seemed only moments ago I was living a content life with friends and a family. I was looking forward to declaring victory and sharing the story of my conquest. In the blink of an eye, all of it had been taken away from me and now I'm here. It was like waking up on the *Planet of the Apes*. Everything was upside down. Everything was . . . wrong.

"If not back home, I should be in Heaven." I declared. "I don't know what all this nonsense is about. But I know, I shouldn't be here. I know that for a fact." I said, feigning confidence.

"Is that so? You are a blind man who doesn't know he cannot see. You refuse to accept the lessons taught. When God created you as a human it was a miraculous gift that allowed you to gain spirituality and understanding. With this gift comes the responsibility to accept what He wants and expects for you, and from you. But time is almost up for you, Louie. Life provided you with an opportunity to demonstrate your virtue and willingness to be with the Lord in His house."

"Well, if that's the case, I should be good to go. I was–"

"I know. A good Catholic. Hold that thought." Karma interrupted.

Trumpets exploded so loudly it vibrated the entire structure. They screamed making their announcement. At the other end of the arena from where I had entered, a door swung open and in walked eleven men and women. Unlike Karma's menacing stature, from a distance, these people appeared more normal in their size. They entered, single file, one behind the other. The man in the lead wore a white robe, similar to the one worn by Karma, and held a stick he used as a walking cane. I could not see the faces of those behind him, but they too were dressed in white. I was still dressed in the camouflage fatigues I wore on my hunting trip. I felt awkward and out of place wearing them; evidence of some wrong doing, but nothing I could do about. The new arrivals moved toward me.

"Who are they?" I asked.

"They are the Deciders. Together, we are the twelve."

B. Lee Baker

The Fifth Chapter

The Deciders' appearance energized the already raging crowd of beasts. I took two conspicuous steps toward Karma. A mistake, if I stopped to think about it. He was clearly not there to offer me sanctuary. But, I felt naked and exposed. The creatures' hate for me was unmistakable. It permeated and soured the air. I wanted to disappear behind him or somehow escape. I looked around and thought about running. I didn't know where I would go, and feared if I tried, the fence precariously holding back the multitude would topple and I would be smothered in an instant. As the Deciders neared the platform, the haphazard hisses and howls coming from the collection of creatures coalesced and coordinated. Millions of animals of every species wailed what sounded like, *"Justitia. Justitia. Justitia."* It started low and slow, but with each step the Deciders took, the cry intensified, becoming louder and more rapid. It sounded Latin, and it sounded like justice, but it was difficult to discern and my memory failed me again, unable to translate for certain. They repeated this over and over. Louder and louder. There was no sign they would tire. In the surreal absurdity of the moment, I was reminded of a television show I watched as a child. The animals talked and sang songs with their human friends. The perfect picture of a utopian garden. The stark difference was that the talking animals here were not nearly as kind or gentle. Here, they were verbally hostile and sneered.

My mouth went dry and could feel an unattractive white crust forming in the corners of my lips. I moved even closer to Karma and whispered a question I thought he might answer,

"What are they chanting?"

"*Justitia.* It means, justice. They demand justice, Louie."

I wondered if the barrage coming from the horde behind the barricade would ever end. It was so difficult to think with the noise. The Deciders remained in single formation on top the platform and moved toward Karma and me. I wanted to know why they demanded justice. Justice for what, but the arrival of the Deciders to the platform whipped up the already electrified crowd into a frenzy. It was the sound of the universe crying out for some unforgiveable, unforgettable act.

Animal Killer

The first of the Deciders to reach the top of platform was the man who led the group from when they first entered the arena. He had long stringy white hair with a matching long white beard. Now that he was closer, I could see he looked very sad. He reminded me of a human version of the *Winter Warlock* from the 1970 television movie, *Santa Claus is Comin' to Town*. He captured my gaze and we locked eyes. His expression turned from sadness to fury. With no warning he charged at me. I tensed and braced myself expecting him to run me over. I took a quick step back, stumbling a bit. He stopped abruptly just before crashing into me. This brought robust cheers from the audience. I clenched my teeth and made a fist. I readied myself for a fight. He never turned his stare and did not blink. He looked directly into my eyes. The crowd was loving the act of aggression and intimidation. They howled. It was deafening.

"My name is Giovanni Francesco di Bernardone."

He spoke with a pronounced distinct northern Italian accent. The accent sounded similar to my father's. He paused as if his name should mean something to me.

"I was the Italian Catholic friar and a preacher remembered as Saint Francis of Assisi."

I took a step back.

"Wha, what? I don't under– What the *hel*–" I finally managed, "I don't believe."

Anyone who attended Catholic school, even dazed and uninterested, knows that Saint Francis is the Patron Saint of animals.

I then knew I was in serious trouble, but I forced myself to relax and unclench. I wasn't about to physically spar with a bona fide Saint. I stood before him in awe. However, he did not allow me to retreat. He stepped forward invading my space and cut me off. He smacked his hands together as if he prepared to pray. They remained stuck together as he began to gyrate them up and down while speaking.

"I'm here to demand justice. I'm here to demand compensation for the blood you shed."

He paused and allowed the crowd to react. They gladly complied, the jeers were deafening.

"For the lives you shattered." Boos and hisses. "For the cruelty you showed." More shouts. "For the pain you caused."

He pointed his shaking finger at me accusingly. Each statement elevating the level of tension.

"I'm here to make sure the other Deciders know exactly who you are. To make sure you receive what you've earned . . . According to your deeds."

Animal Killer

As he spoke, the other Deciders each sat on the stone chairs in the middle of the dais. Each wore perfect, pristine, radiant white robes. My blood pressure increased causing my heart to beat wildly. Perspiration formed around my forehead and neck, and then dripped down my back. As abruptly as Saint Francis had come at me, he spun and walked away toward the identical chair facing mine. With his back to me, he threw his right arm above his head to accentuate and further demonstrate the level of his disgust and bellowed, "*Echh!*"

When he reached his seat, he turned and caught my gaze, letting out, "*Hmpf!*" Further emphasizing his revulsion. He then dropped hard into the seat waiting to receive him.

Karma turned from Saint Francis, looked at me for a moment, and then turned to the Deciders and nodded. The crowd noise hushed to a murmur.

The first Decider, seated on the far left, rose to her feet. She was a portly woman, but beautiful. She looked a bit nervous.

"I am the Teacher."

Her long hair rolled into a bun at the back of her head, held together by a purple ribbon.

"I did all I could to teach you all I knew."

She bit her lip and sat down.

The man sitting next to her rose, and like Karma, he was a physical specimen. He looked like he had been carved from stone.

"I am Fate. I forged the places and events where your being was meant to be and experience." He said confidently.

I thought to myself, *what an interesting turn of phrase, where my being was meant to be. What about where my being is to be? Had something changed*, I wondered.

An equally impressive man sitting beside Fate stood.

"I am Free Will. I make sure no one forces you to do anything you do not want to do. It's all on you. Always has been. Always will be."

Each then took a turn to introduce themselves.

"I am the Past. I helped create the life you lived."

"I am the Present. I am helping create the life you are experiencing now."

"I am the Future. I am influencing events to make the life you should have."

"I am Hope. I do what I can to show you there is something better waiting for you."

"I am Faith. I encourage you to believe, no matter the storm you encounter, no matter what you see, no matter what you're told."

"I am Wisdom. You would have been well served to seek me more."

"I am the Maker of Opposites. I make certain there is a yin to every yang. Without an opposite, nothing would have any significance or context."

Then the last *Decider* stood. She was almost too beautiful to absorb, she glowed with perfection, and radiated comfort.

"I am Love. I have loved you from the beginning. No matter what you did. I will always love you. No matter what you will do, I will love you. I experience love through you. When you didn't know what love was, I tried to tell you, show you. I wish there had been more."

I had no satisfying response, but looking at her, the heckling and screaming mob melted away. I wanted to embrace her, to be close to her. When she spoke, there was no worry, perfect bliss enveloped me. I received a glimpse of paradise. Then, ripped away, the feeling fled the moment she sat down. The shouts from the crowd immediately exploded into my ears and panic returned.

Karma looked to me,

"Sit!"

He motioned with his hand toward the seat. Karma remained standing. He continued,

"Each of us has played a vital role in your life. Each will have a say. These are special beings, created by the Lord. Great spiritual forces to help you, to help all souls, become the beings each were meant to be. But, in the end, it is up to you. Free Will makes certain of that."

He turned to acknowledge Free Will, and continued, "He keeps the others in check."

Free Will nodded in agreement. Karma moved toward the front of the platform and surveyed the masses.

"Ultimately, no matter what these forces do to push and prod, the decision to be or not to be what God wants for you, and from you, is up to you and you alone. You alone will enjoy the benefits and suffer the burdens of your decisions."

It was difficult to concentrate. I became increasingly concerned and focused on Saint Francis' scathing accusations and cry for justice. I feared the Saint's charges, along with Karma's emphasis on free will, were harbingers of my future. As a lawyer, I never considered it wise or good practice to permit accusations to remain unchallenged. I was eager to respond. Karma quickly spun to me,

"Ask your question."

This was my opening. I was not going down without a fight. I was done being a passive observer to this kangaroo court and needed to fight back.

"Fate forged the events I experienced and ultimate place for my being?"

"Yes." Karma confirmed.

"Well, if that is the case, how could I do anything to change what he has already preordained? How can you be angry with anything I did? Blame Fate, not me." I said and pointed to Fate.

"You alone are responsible for your actions, Louie. Free Will made certain you could choose to follow or ignore the will of God."

"That makes no sense. These are contrary. Either my destiny was predetermined or I had the ability to do anything, go anywhere, be anyone. You cannot have it both ways."

I was immensely proud of my response. The mental gymnastics backed Karma into a corner. If Fate already determined the outcome, I was blameless for any infraction these Deciders believed I may have committed. As far as I saw it, they could not have it both ways. Either free will meant whatever I did was mine to own, or fate had already decided what was to become of me, no matter my actions.

"It is a silly notion that fate and free will cannot coexist. There is always an opposite," he said, turning to acknowledge the Maker of Opposites. "You've heard the story of the man and the storm."

He did not pause to allow me to respond.

"It perfectly illustrates how free will and fate both exist in the same place. A man had a dream and was told a bad storm would destroy his village. But the man was also assured that God would protect him. Just as he dreamed, the next day, a storm descended on his town. On the first day of the storm the man's brother fled, but first visits the man to warn him to leave the village with him. But, this faithful man refused his brother's help. He replied that God will protect him. On the second day of the storm, a neighbor fleeing the town passed his home and offered to rescue him. But again, this man refused help, replying that he was sure God would protect him. On the third day, the waters rose so high the man had to flee to his roof. A town official passed the drowning home on a boat and offered to take the man to safety. Again, the man refused, having faith, he was certain God would protect him. Soon after, the man drowned and died. In Heaven, he asked God: Why didn't you help me as you promised? God replied: I sent your brother, your neighbor, and even an official in boat; but you refused to accept them." He paused to allow me to consider the story before continuing. "As demonstrated by this story, it was the man's fate to be saved, but Free Will made certain he had the option to reject his destiny, in this case, his rescue. Similarly for you, Louie, you have been taught the word of God by the Teacher. Fate has reserved a place for you in the Kingdom of Heaven, but how did you exercise what Free Will afforded you? How did you choose? We shall see."

I looked down, like a child who had just been caught in a lie. I was verbally sparring with a man who'd had this very conversation a trillion times. He was prepared. I was not. I turned my attention to Saint Francis who was outwardly restless, almost in distress. His right knee rocked up and down while he waited his turn. It took all his intestinal fortitude to restrain himself, anxious to stand and have his say. I could not imagine what I had done to anger him so much. What sway did he have with the Deciders? I felt like an attorney from out of state going up against the local guy who played poker and drank beer with the judge every Friday night. It was so cliché. As the outsider, how could I possibly hope to get a fair shake? I turned to Love, hoping to escape and recede back into the bliss she offered. The feeling wouldn't return. She wouldn't, or couldn't, look at me. Karma then turned to Saint Francis. This was his cue.

The Saint shot up from his seat. He moved away from its wooden confines and deliberately stalked around the platform. He paused before saying anything, but paced back and forth methodically surveying the crowd. He waited, as great orators do, building the suspense. The onlookers accommodated, the noise reduced to a quiet hush.

They all waited with the anticipation that had been building, but somehow contained, just waiting to discharge and explode. He seemed to make eye contact with every single one of the millions attending, moving to and fro on the stage. He wanted them to know what he was about to say was meant for each of them. That every word mattered. When he finally spoke, his voice boomed.

"*Fiat Justitia*– let justice be done!" He cried.

The crowd exploded. It was a massive release of pent up anger of unimaginable measure. They had been waiting for it to be said. They resumed their mantra, "*Justitia. Justitia. Justitia.*" I quickly learned it was more than agitation, and that Saint Francis' aggressive body language when meeting me was actually restrained. I began to fear things were worse than I had first suspected. I wanted to know where the sympathy was for me. I had just been killed by my own son. I lost my family. Everything I cared about was gone. I questioned, how a fellow *paisan* and Saint of the Church, who had never met me, could treat me like this. Particularly, because on many occasions I had prayed to many Saints. Maybe not this Saint in particular, but to others. I looked down to the floor. Disappointment and swelling despair did not adequately describe the feeling. It was suffocating.

Animal Killer

How did I get to this place? I remained in disbelief that this spectacle was meant for me alone.

The Saint turned to me, "Luigi."

I hated being called Luigi. My grandparents called me Luigi. I loved my grandparents, but despite my pleas for them to stop, they never wavered. My friends, unfortunately, overheard this one time. It took months for them to drop calling me Luigi from a popular video game that had flooded the arcades at the time. Every day they asked me, *where's your brother, Luigi?* They thought that was a real hoot.

Saint Francis continued, "Review of the life is mandated by the Creator. The destruction of a soul is the most serious judgment that may be rendered. Know, I do not hate you. To the contrary, I once loved you very much. I had high hopes for you."

This prompted harsh heckles from the audience.

"Nooo!" An animal shouted.

"He is the devil!" Said another.

"He murdered my mother!" Shouted another.

Saint Francis paused to permit the crowd members to unleash, and then continued.

"But, look around. Look at those gathered here. Listen to their stories and pleas. I'm here for them. Not you!"

He turned to the onlookers who hung on his every word.

"No, friends. I don't hate him personally." He then quickly wheeled around to me, pointing his finger at my chest like a loaded handgun, "But I do despise what you've done to them!" He swung his arm and opened his hand to the masses. "And, what you've done to the most Holy One above."

He shouted, making a fist with his open hand, but for his index finger which he thrusted up, pointing to the sky. This quieted the agitated animals a bit.

My mind recoiled. The scene was an unrelenting, unimaginable, assault.

Saint Francis continued.

"I am here to make the record. To state the obvious. To say out loud what everyone here already knows, or should know. To say what the Creator knows. And to say those words which by now, you Luigi, even if you won't admit it, what you should know too. I see no path to the Kingdom for you. We've tried and tried and tried. You consistently failed and disappointed. It is time to end you."

He turned to the Deciders and spoke more evenly,

"*Miei amici*. My friends. We must do what God requires. We should learn from this, Luigi. We should mourn him. But, it is time for this one to go. His crimes are too great. Giving him another chance will result in the shedding of more innocent blood. Allowing him into the Kingdom would be abhorrent and contrary to God's will. We cannot and should not permit this."

He then turned back to me, again pointing his finger. This time it was aimed at my head and we locked eyes. His voice again boomed like thunder.

"I assert you have offended the Creator. You've dismissed His will. I charge you have committed crimes against the Lord and, therefore, are not worthy to enter into the Kingdom of Heaven."

"*Whoa*. Hold on there!"

I could not hold back. I jumped out of my seat. Fear and self-preservation kicked in. I had been suppressing the reality of my circumstances, but I suddenly understood, I needed to defend my soul.

"I committed no crime." I pronounced with absolute certainty. "I have been a good Catholic. I do not belong here. You have it all wrong. I may not know much, but I know I believed in Jesus and went to church." *At least on the important holidays*, I thought to myself. "I never violated God's will nor committed any crime." I said confidently.

"You presume to deny the wisdom of this council?" Saint Francis challenged. He clenched his teeth and fist. "You hurl toward your destruction without accepting responsibility. You refuse to repent for your sins. You make the case easy."

The Sixth Chapter

Before I could fully respond to the Saint's prophetically threatening indictment, Karma interrupted.

"We are here to determine if you are good to go, as you say, Louie. The world is perfectly imperfect. Created by God to provide all beings with immeasurable opportunities, big and small, to demonstrate their willingness to abide by His word. To do as much good as you can, for as long as you can, for as many as you can. Did you do that? Did you do all you could for others? Or, did you seek your own fulfillment and glory? Did you help those who could do nothing for you in return? Did you love, all of your neighbors, in all the forms you found them?"

He paused for a response.

"Yes I did! I took care of my family! I loved my family. Where I come from that means something. You may want to convict me of some offense, but I went to confession. I was absolved of my sins! I put money in the collection plate. That helped others. So don't tell me I wasn't a good person, if that's what you're implying. Was I perfect? Probably not. Who is? Was I required to be perfect?"

"Perfect? No. You were not required to be perfect." He said shaking his head. "As I've said before, perfect in spirit is what is expected. Perfection in your intention, in your desires, that is what we are considering. Try as you might to defend yourself, your words cannot hide what your heart shouts and your actions confess. Not from us. Yes, of course, you did some good. For some. You took care of your family. But, that is not the extent of God's will. Do you think you can confess some of your wrongs, but obtain absolution for them all? You don't get deliverance from the wrongs you did not, or would not, acknowledge. There is no liberation from the evil you willfully embrace. Absolution comes only to those who acknowledge their mistakes, repent, and turn from their wicked ways."

I opened my mouth, but was cut off.

"Before you protest or try to make the case otherwise, remember, I am Karma. I am not here to be persuaded of anything. There is no passion or prejudice with me. I only recognize what was, what is, and what should be. Likewise, the Deciders are not here to be persuaded. They too recognize what was, what is, and what should be. All the good. All the bad. All the indifference. You either fulfilled God's will or you did not. There are no excuses here. No explanations."

I was being tag teamed by one guy that hated me and by another one who seemed he could care less what happened to me.

"So I am being persecuted for not being Mother Theresa."

The arena erupted in laughter. I smiled, figuring I just scored a point. I took the opportunity to attack.

"Where is my defense? I still don't know what exactly I did wrong. I demand to know!"

Saint Francis turned red. Shockingly, Karma seemed to change a shade or two darker. I pushed it too far. My stomach churned and my pulse again quickened. I felt nauseous. The stench from the crowd didn't help either. The barrage continued as Saint Francis took over.

"Mother Theresa! The best defense you offer, is that you took care of your family! Well– congratulations. You did the bare minimum, a far cry from Mother Theresa," he said, while his fingers pinched together as if holding salt, while he shook his hand. He continued.

"Good for you. Guess what? God commands that you be good to all His creations. Not just your family." He then motioned to the crowd. "The Earth. The people. The birds. The animals. From the ant to the elephant. The fish in the sea and the creatures that crawled upon the land. And yes, Animal Killer, that includes the deer too. A real favorite of yours, we know."

"What are you saying exactly?" I interrupted. "What is my crime? I want to know specifically. What are my offenses against God as you say? I want to–"

"You hunted and killed God! And you did it for fun. God is in all creation. He gives part of Himself to every soul. Every living thing. And you hunted them. Stuffed them. Mounted them on your wall. A conqueror of God."

"Stop," I said, raising my hands. "I hunted God? I don't think so. You got it wrong. Yes, I hunted animals. What's wrong with hunting animals?"

"It's not just the hunting you did. It's what your heart speaks. Your contempt. Why do you think God's animals are any less important than man? Like man, when you kick an animal it hurts. Starve an animal it pains. Injure an animal it bleeds. Ignore and show indifference toward an animal in need and you crush its soul leaving it to wither and die. Each creature you so carelessly killed, maimed and ignored, contained the soul of God. He gave a piece of Himself to each breathing creature. When you inflict your cruelty upon them, you do these things to God Himself! You believe because an animal does not speak your language that it has no soul? That the Lord does not care? That there won't be retribution for what you've done to them?"

"God doesn't condemn hunting." I pronounced.

"Wrong, Luigi, wrong. Kindness and love toward all is a fundamental and basic precondition of being with the Lord. You cannot be with God if you do not love God. You cannot love God if you do not love His creations. It is through His creations that He expresses who He is. It is through His creations you reveal who you are. If you are unkind toward any of His creations why would He allow you into the Kingdom of Heaven? God created the Earth and all the creatures in it so that they all could one day come dwell in the Kingdom with Him. Expand its boundless beauty. Not corrupt it with the likes of you! A perfect place where every creature could demonstrate love and worthiness. That's why only perfection of spirit may enter. I have been blessed by the Lord. Entrusted to protect His creatures. I have no choice, but to demand justice for them. To protect them."

"Was I not supposed to eat? I ate what I hunted. Hunting to survive is a crime?"

He turned to the crowd, still addressing me,

"I ate what I hunted." He slowly repeated. "He lies too! He lies to us. He lies to himself." He spun around again, pointing that finger at me. "Admit it Animal Killer. Admit what you did!"

"I'm not lying. There's nothing to admit."

"*Basta! Enough!* Just stop! You did not hunt for food. You did not hunt out of necessity. You had supermarkets. You had other sources of food. Vegetables to eat. You hunted and mounted your conquests on your wall. You bragged about it. You received a perverted rush from destroying a living breathing creature created by God. And what about the animals you killed that you did not eat? There were plenty of those. *Huhhh? Hmmm?* What about them, Animal Killer?"

I had no compelling rebuttal. I looked down and mumbled,

"I don't know how I got here."

He finally unclenched his fist and his face softened. The crowd sensed this and shouted, voicing their disapproval. He continued.

"You want to know how you ended up here? Like countless others, you chased the pleasures of the flesh. You fed your ego. Concerned yourself with your stature. All the while you starved your soul. You went to church, but tuned out the message. You rejected God. You preferred to live by your own code of conduct. Ignoring God's will."

"Untrue. This is so unfair." I said shaking my head in disbelief.

He lowered his voice.

"Luigi. Listen to me. *Più di cinquemila anni*. For more than five thousand years the most Holy One has tried to teach man. To love. To be kind. To be fair and merciful. He carved His Commandments in stone. He gave His law to Moses who wrote His will on a scroll. This was the God given instruction manual for life. No one who read it, or heard it, could claim they did not know. It was simple. Follow its direction and you will be welcomed into the Kingdom of Heaven. Ignore it, and suffer the consequences. Time and again Karma would be called on to deliver justice because so many ignored the word. When so few demonstrated perfection of spirt and were cast to Oblivion, God found Heaven a lonely place. He was wounded. His people refused to choose good and kindness instead of evil and selfishness. So the Creator tried again. He sent His Son from His house in the Kingdom to be a living example. To be the word of God incarnate. And, to be a willing sacrifice to cover the shortcomings of those willing to try to fulfill the desires of the Holy One. His message expanded, this became the Holy Bible, that book you held and supposedly lived by. The message was made even more clear and concise. Be good to each other and every creature created by the Lord. Follow his Commandments. Believe in Him and follow His Son's example. Do so, and enter the Kingdom. Ignore it, and perish. You know all of this. You chose to ignore it. It angers me to hear people say, 'There is no God.' Imagine a world where no one followed His word, where kindness and compassion did not exist. A world where each individual decided right and wrong. Is that the world you would prefer, for you and your family?"

"Thanks for the sermon." I cracked. "What does this have to do with me?"

"Take heed of your tone, Animal Killer. You are about to be fed to your final and ultimate destruction," he warned.

"Look. I was good a person. God never said hunting was wrong."

Saint or no Saint, this guy was pushing my buttons. I never liked being threatened.

"The Holy Book is filled with message after message requiring kindness. Sport hunting is not kindness. The Lord created the birds of the air, the fish of the sea, and the creatures of the Earth *before* he created man. The Lord entrusted His creation and His creatures to man. He never relinquished ownership over them, but merely provided guardianship to man over them. How did you ever come to the conclusion that the creatures He made were not important to Him? That you would not be held to account? You attended church week after week, holding that Holy Book and walked out considering yourself a man of God. But every day in between you violated Commandment after Commandment. You ignored the word of the Lord. You went about living life ignoring the Lord's will! And still, you claim to be a good man. You hypocrite!"

"One second. I repeat, the Bible says nothing about hunting or being mean to animals is a violation of God's law. There's nothing wrong with killing animals."

"And the fact that this is your belief is all we need to send you to Oblivion."

"Why? I'm no priest. I don't have the theological education you obviously have, but with all respect, you are wrong! God encouraged animal sacrifices. And, he gave man, uh . . . that's me . . . control over the Earth and all things on it. He specifically ordered us to kill animals and now you convict me of killing animals."

My response sparked new hope within me. I didn't know why I hadn't thought of animal sacrifices earlier. My legal training and trial experience intervened and spurred me on. I remembered the words of wisdom from a law school professor who advised, that as a lawyer, when you have the law on your side, argue the law. When you have the facts on your side, argue the facts. And, when you don't have either, just argue!

The crowd roared in disapproval.

"Oh, Luigi, how I pray for you. You have learned nothing. Countless hours in church, and you know nothing. You could not be more distant from God than you are this very moment. *Ignorantia non excusat!*" He hollered to the crowd and then turned to me, "Your ignorance is no excuse! It will not save you. If you had taken the time to know the Creator, instead of chasing material pleasures, you would have learned a thing or two. Had you taken the time to actually read the Holy Book and understand it, you would know that there was a time God commanded the sacrifice of specific animals. Animals rare and scarce. The sacrifice was meant to be a demonstration of submission to the will of God, and request for forgiveness for misdeeds. Animal slaughter was not ordained to fulfill some self-serving need to impress, or satisfy the thirst for dominance and power."

"Still, I'm right. God ordered animal killings."

"*Stupida*. No, Luigi. For God to accept the sacrifice, the animal had to first be the property of the one making the sacrifice. They had to know the animal. It was not a random, indiscriminate, purposeless kill. The animal was important to the person, either for food or commerce. Otherwise it was not a sacrifice or a loss. It was about the person's willingness to give up something of value to God as a sign, a payment for their sins. The animal had to be spotless and without blemish. How many of those do you suppose existed? The sacrificial rules made it so difficult to follow, that the true purpose was to teach man not to sin. God loved these sacrificed animals. They hold a special place in the Kingdom and have been rewarded for their sacrifice. You didn't butcher these animals to cover your sins. They were not important to you. You felt no pain and loss when you slaughtered them. Don't for a minute think you can stand here and defend yourself by justifying your slaughter. That your killings are somehow comparable to the supreme sacrifice offered by honorable men under the old covenant looking to obtain forgiveness for their wrongs. We know better, Luigi."

The crowd hissed.

What could I say to all of this? I feared he might be right. At the least, I was losing the debate. My fear began to transform into dread.

"Had you paid any attention in church, you'd know God sent His Son to be slaughtered in the place of those animal sacrifices. His blood, in place of theirs, was meant to wash away all the sins of man. What did you do, Luigi? You continued to slaughter, stalk and persecute the animals for your pleasure. The countless souls lost because of this lack of compassion and flawed thinking." He said, shaking his head disapprovingly.

My will to continue to battle began to fade, but I countered, "I'd love to know where in the Bible says to be good to animals."

The crowd disgusted, erupted again.

Saint Francis was ready, he didn't hesitate.

"'A righteous man has regard for the life of his animal.' Proverbs twelve, verse ten. Read it! God commands you and your animals to rest on the Sabbath. That's Exodus twenty, verse ten. God commands that you help your enemies' animal that has fallen under too heavy a burden. This appears twice in Exodus twenty three, verse five and Deuteronomy twenty two, verse four. Did not God speak directly to the animals when he commanded them to board the ark of Noah? He didn't do that just to keep them alive so you'd have something to kill for fun."

He paused again, waiting for an answer that would not come, then he continued.

"'Let every created thing give praise to the Lord, for he issued his command, and they came into

94

being.' Psalm one hundred forty eight, verse five. This was not a unique command to man alone, but *every* created thing was directed to give praise."

The animals roared in approval. I looked at them, feeling vulnerable and insignificant.

"When God first created the world, what did he say? 'I now give you every seed-bearing plant on the face of the entire earth and every tree that has fruit with seed in it. They will be yours for food,'" he yelled, spit spewing from his mouth, before continuing. "'And to all the animals of the earth, and to every bird of the air, and to all the creatures that move on the ground – everything that has the breath of life in it – I give every green plant for food.' You'll find that nugget in the very first chapter of the very first book. He did not say, eat the animals, I created them for you! This was what God originally wanted for you. Yes, He temporarily modified this command after the flood, for His reasons, but He never said go and destroy the animals for fun. He never said, go butcher and neglect My creations. So, explain, where in that perverted wicked mind of yours do you derive that God doesn't care about the animals, that they were created for your pleasure."

"I didn't know."

"You didn't know because you didn't care to know. What about the words of the Son, to whom you worshiped and prayed? He told the world to not fear for their own well-being. That God's love is revealed all around them. He preached that His Father feeds all the birds of the air and that not one will ever fall to the ground dead without Him knowing. You can find that one in Mathew six, verse twenty six and ten, and ten, verse twenty nine. Does that indicate God did not care about them? I think not. 'The earth is the Lord's, and all it contains, the world, and those who dwell in it.' Psalm twenty four, verse one. You ignored that one too."

He paused making his case.

"The creations of God were not meant to be trophies. The Fourth Commandment, thou shall not kill. You can't claim you never heard that one. God never limited the command to refrain from murdering only humans. That was man's corruption of the command. I could go on and on and on. Despite these clear and repeated directives, you instead chose to follow your own pleasures. Your perverse desires. Your murders were not offerings to God, pleas to forgive you of your sins. You didn't do it to avoid starvation. Yet, you come before us and declare yourself worthy to enter the Kingdom. I say no, Luigi. I say *no!* And, based on everything I have seen, I say *never!* I say, *Fiat Justitia*– let justice be done!"

Animal Killer

His words echoed throughout the arena, condemning me.

B. Lee Baker

The Seventh Chapter

A wave of emotions overtook me. The cry for justice inflicted a mortal wound to my soul. I became sickened with terror as a guttural fear gushed from my bowels. I had no idea what his demand for justice would mean for me. I became very cold, and shivered uncontrollably. I cupped my hands and blew into them, trying to warm them. The possibility I would be sent to Oblivion, of never seeing those I loved again, of being nothing without any thoughts, obliterated, was simply too much to endure. *All because I hunted?* It was all too surreal. Throughout my life I listened with complete passiveness to the warnings of Hell. I dismissed the forewarnings through various rationalizations: It was not a real place. It didn't apply to me because I had been baptized and believed Jesus was the Christ. Hell was used to control people. There were many others as well.

Almost as bad as the fear of Oblivion itself, was the worry I felt beginning to crawl just below the surface of my skin. Worry for the punishment they would see fit to deal me for what they say I had done. No matter how hard I tried to remain positive, my mind returned to one thought. *He shall render to each according to his works*. I suppressed the concern. I was a good man. I knew that. Still, this guy really had it out for me.

Saint Francis, facing the spectators, continued, "How did this being use his time? He disobeyed the Lord's Commandments. He lived with a hard heart. He offered no compassion. He literally hunted down the Lord's love incarnate." He turned to the Deciders who all sat stoically. "On behalf of all those persecuted by this being, we demand justice. We must have justice. But, we are not masochists. How many times must we watch Karma distribute his works that inevitably produce suffering? And, all these efforts just to bring this being back into balance, only to then watch him fall yet again. We have seen it before. Not all can be saved."

"I didn't know! I did nothing wrong!" I screamed. I would not accept this attack on my character any longer. "I want to go back. I want to see my wife! Right now! Enough already. Have some mercy."

Animal Killer

"Which is it, Luigi? You did nothing wrong, or you didn't know?" Saint Francis, asked contemptuously. "You've heard nothing I've said. *Idiota!* This is not about hunting. This is about what dwells and reigns in your heart. This is about how you treated the innocent. How you felt, and still feel about them. At this very moment, you still resist to account and repent for your crimes against the Holy One. You spit in the face of God and plea for peace. You defiled His creations, but now beg for mercy. Where was their mercy?" He motioned to the crowd. The masses hollered in agreement. "You offered no mercy to them. To the most vulnerable. To those who most needed it. You want understanding, but indiscriminately inflicted your butchery. You offered no understanding. You want justice, but you gave none. You want safety, but offered no quarter to those you attacked. I have offered the words of God, but you still refuse to accept them. You deny responsibility. You claim ignorance. You fail to repent. You dismiss your actions while you discount their value."

"All I can say is, I'm sorry. I didn't know. I cannot believe you want to obliterate me because I hunted? They're just animals, for Christ sake!"

More howling from the crowd.

"End him!" One animal called out.

"Oblivion!" Shouted another.

The fence clanged and rocked even more violently. I was certain it was going to collapse under their constant barrage.

The Saint pressed on, solidifying his case.

"They are just animals." He repeated my words. He turned to the Deciders. "Does anything else need to be said?" He turned his back to me, "No part of the purpose of your life included killing or cruelty. You've suffered a paralysis of the soul. You no longer feel all you should. Spin it however you like, Luigi, in the end, you are the destroyer of the innocent. You're the Animal Killer. You get to decide who lives and who dies. You're above it all. You think the Creator wants someone who receives fulfillment from such perversity to dwell with Him in His Kingdom?" And your defense, is that you were good to your family. That you ate some of what you killed. That you didn't know. That about sums it up?"

He looked at me with disgust. There was nothing more for me to say.

"I am here to make sure the Deciders know what is what. I am here to make sure you get the justice you have coming to you. You're just lucky it's not my call."

With that, Saint Francis finished and sat down. He folded his arms. His face red with rage, he wouldn't look at me. If his words left any doubt how he felt on the subject of my continued existence, his body language filled in the blanks.

Karma moved close to me and leaned over the railing encircling me. I felt like a war criminal confined to his tiny suffocating chamber. The only detail missing was the bullet proof glass encasing me in. Beyond its confines, the world judged. The conviction, a forgone conclusion. He whispered into my ear,

"Now the hard part begins, Louie. God requires justice. No more, no less."

This again reenergized the crowd. They resumed the chant, "*Justitia. Justitia. Justitia.*" They were there for vengeance. Nothing less would satisfy or satiate them.

"No matter what is decided, before you move on, go back, or suffer banishment in Oblivion, Karma demands you experience the consequences of your deeds. There is no other way. We must determine what exactly is due. We call this the *Review.*" The throngs of creatures there to witness my demise erupted again.

"I do not want you to think of what comes next as a punishment. It has yet to be determined if you are to receive justice that requires suffering. That will come. This is rather an opportunity to learn God's will. To take the experience with you. Wherever that may be."

He tapped my forehead with his finger. In that moment, all control was arrested from me, if I ever really had any. My eyes were forced closed. I became paralyzed as time froze.

Somehow, I was eleven years old again. I was sitting on the stoop in front of my house with my best friend, Mikey. He lived next door. The high summer sun baked us as we readied ourselves for a day of playing and getting into trouble on the concrete jungle of Brooklyn. I could tell he was just dying to tell me some news.

Finally, he shared the big announcement,

"I got a second Tom Seaver."

"No way."

"Yep. My dad brought me home a pack and he was right on top."

He knew this was a real blow. I was a diehard Met fan. Mikey and I competed with each other every summer to see which of us could collect all the players of our favorite team's baseball cards first. He was a Yankee fan and had been trying to swindle me out of my Reggie Jackson card. I knew this was going to be a difficult negotiation. I would have to give up my Reggie card in a trade for Tom Terrific. Nothing less would suffice. At least it would be a fair trade.

For anyone other than the marquee players, rather than trade, we would flip for them. Flipping cards became a sport in and of itself. We would toss a card in the air and it would land heads or tails. We spent hours perfecting our techniques so that we could toss a card and direct it to land face up or down at will. If you could match your opponent, you got his card, if you didn't, he got yours. Once I caught Mikey's brother, Sal, cheating by gluing two cards together. This insured he would always have a head or tail. I learned my lesson after being swindled a time or two and knew better than to flip with any of them. A trade would at least guarantee I would get something for the give.

We left the confines of the stoop and went out to patrol our street. Walking our block, corner to corner, the negotiation commenced. The bartering was short lived because we stumbled upon a large ant colony. This was quite common on our street. We loved messing with them. The ants created a dirt mound above a gap in the concrete of the sidewalk. In the center was a hole that allowed the ants access in and out of their underground city. Mikey kicked at the dirt and covered the hole. We thought that was real fun. Watching the ants scramble and go to work replacing the mound.

"Hey– you got any Lysol in your house?" Mikey asked.

"How would I know?"

"Go check. I'm going to go get my brother's lighter. I'm going to show you something really cool. Meet you back here in two minutes."

We both took off running to our respective homes. I ran inside and checked under our kitchen sink and grabbed a can of Lysol. Mikey ran and got his brother's lighter, neatly hidden under his mattress. We were back at the colony minutes later.

"Ok, I am going to put the flame near the opening. You spray the can right towards the flame. Make sure you don't point it at me."

"Why?"

"You'll see."

After several tries, Mikey got the lighter to ignite.

"Go ahead. Spray it. What are you waiting for? An engraved invitation?"

I pressed the button at the top of the canister and was doused with Lysol.

"*Haaaa!* You have to point it in the right direction, *stunod!*"

Embarrassed, I turned the can and sprayed. The mist ignited as it passed the flame. The ball of fire sped toward the colony, engulfing and incinerating everything in its path.

In that instant, as the flame travelled, my perspective changed. I was transported inside the colony. I was one of the ants. I looked around. Stunned at first. I was surrounded by hundreds of ants. Suddenly, bodies were moving toward me. Ants trampling on top of one another, running deeper underground. It happened in a flash. I was consumed by the sequential combination of the suffocating stink of disinfectant, followed by the heat, and finished by the fireball. My exoskeleton burned and cracked before it began to melt. The screams and cries came from all directions. The heat so great, it fused hundreds of the melting skeletons together while many were still alive. The pain and agony immense. As the colony burned, the stench of rotten blue cheese overtook the nest. At the time, as an eleven year old boy, this was fun. I had no idea. Experiencing it now, I could feel the impact of the mass murder. In the moment, they were no longer just ants. My life faded in horror watching the other ants around me cling to one another as their bodies melted.

Everything went dark.

I was still shuddering from the calamity I had just experienced when I awoke. I had been burned alive and watched so many around me also burn and scream in agony. I could still feel it. Still hear it. The smell of the rotten blue cheese remained inside my nasal passages, even though I was now a long way from that massacre. I was thirteen. This time, it was not me as the thirteen year old on the baseball diamond having fun and smelling hotdogs, but rather I was in my cousin's backyard in Jersey. New Jersey wasn't like Brooklyn where everyone knew how to mind their own business. So we walked deep behind the property. It was fall and the decaying leaves were dropping from the large red oak trees that littered the property. My father handed me the pistol.

"Go ahead, take it. It's not loaded." He said forcefully. "Squeeze. Squeeze the trigger. Practice keeping it steady while you apply constant pressure." He said through the cigarette that dangled from his lips and smoke irritating his squinting eyes.

I took the gun and started snapping the trigger back in successive motions as fast as I could. The smack to the back of my head knocked me into a pile of leaves face first. No matter how accustomed I became to my father's smacks, I never knew when they would come, so they startled me every time. The force of the hit usually sent me sprawling. What compounded the blow was that his hands had calloused and hardened. They were brick-like weapons, the product of a lifetime of hard labor, capable of causing serious damage.

"This is not a toy!" He yelled.

He didn't bother to help me up, but reached for the pistol. He pointed to it.

"This is the safety. When it is on like this, it will not fire. You have to push this to release the safety. Only take off the safety when you are going to shoot. Only shoot when you mean to practice or kill. Now try again."

After some time, when he was satisfied I wouldn't kill myself or him, he took the gun and showed me how to load it. Then he handed it back to me.

"There. Over there, those squirrels. Practice on them."

He pointed to two squirrels. I watched them chase each other around the trees.

"No poppa. I don't want to."

"*Shhhhh.* It's ok. This is what our family does. Where do you think all that food you eat comes from?"

"No. I don't eat squirrels."

He slapped me in the back of my head again.

"It's practice. Real men hunt. All the men in our family hunt. It will do more for you than that stupid baseball."

I raised the pistol, closed my eyes, and slowly squeezed the trigger the way my father demanded. The explosion of the bullet startled the squirrels, but not enough to chase them away. A chunk of the tree and bark fanned about in different directions. They continued their game of tag with one another. The clap of the bullet frightened me as well, but I thankfully managed to hold onto the gun.

"Again." He muffled through his pursed lips still sucking on his cigarette.

Another shot. This time, when I pulled the trigger, time slowed. I had an out of body experience. I was transported into one of the two squirrels. I was on the side of the tree chasing the other squirrel. I felt warm and so happy. I heard its every thought. We were foraging for food and playing along the way. The loud crack of the gun startled me. I looked and saw myself and my father standing several feet away. Before I could think or move, the bullet hit me. The projectile moved so fast it singed my fur and burnt my skin. It exited my body and wedged itself in the tree, but not before partially severing my spinal cord and exploding several organs along the way. I fell to the ground. The pain, initially was all consuming, but paralysis quickly imprisoned me. I looked upon the other squirrel who returned my death gaze. Pain and fear danced in her eyes. I wanted to yell run, but I was dead in seconds.

The thirteen year old boy that had been me, stood there watching with his mouth frozen wide open.

"You got the bastard. Good boy." My father said excitedly.

Animal Killer

The scene played exactly as it had decades ago. I remembered as the horror of the kill faded and was replaced with the pride and approval of my father. I smiled from ear to ear. Seeing this now, I felt revulsion. One minute they were playing with one another, not bothering anyone, and the next, one mate destroyed in a violent and unprovoked attack. The other squirrel ran leaving her dead partner behind. It was the first animal I killed. Everything went dark.

I woke up eighteen years old. I was driving my father's pickup truck. It was the summer between high school and college. My friends Mikey and Tommy were in the car with me.

Laughing, my friend Tommy encouraged me, "speed up. I dare you to take that fucking cat out."

"Nah. Look, it has a collar. Probably someone's pet." I said.

"Don't be such a girl." Tommy provoked.

I pushed down on the gas a little harder. In that instant, I was again transported. I was the cat running across the road. I heard every one of its thoughts. He was searching for food. He was very hungry and weak. His companion had just birthed a number of kittens and was holed up in an abandoned dirty warehouse protecting them and trying to nurse, but food was scarce. As the cat, I turned and saw the car speeding toward me and looked ahead. In that split second I could tell there was no way I was going to make it. *How are they going to make it?* He thought. Sadness washed over me. The tire hit and rolled me under it. It was hot and hard. My body crunched under the tire as it forced all of the air out of my lungs. My organs were crushed and pierced by my broken and splintered bones that punctured though my skin. Unbearable excruciating pain marked the moments I had left. I was unable to respire and began to suffocate. Gasping for air, my mouth opened, trying to suck in air, but none would come. My tongue dangled out of my mouth onto the dirty pavement. While my blood supply was all but cut off, the nerves from the broken bones continued to register the agony. A minute ago I was searching for food for my kittens, and now I was dying. They would never know what happened to me. *Would they think I abandoned them to die?* I tried to lift my head and move to get someone to notice. No one did. I begged for a car to hit me to end the agony. The heat and wind from the passing vehicles brushed hard against me as I lay stuck to the scorching tar road, soaked in my blood and other bodily fluids. Thankfully, darkness quickly consumed me.

The onslaught continued. I woke up in Kenya, Africa. I was on a special private paid safari. The most expensive trip I had ever taken. It was a gift to myself for turning thirty-five. At the time, I had been convinced it was worth every penny.

"You're sure this is enough to make it okay?" I asked.

"Yes. Yes. Everything ok. Very good. We go, we go now." My tour guide responded.

We entered the beat up jeep that struggled to start and headed deeper into the preserve. I wondered if they had a contingency plan if the vehicle stalled or refused to restart. I feared there was none. We drove about an hour with the windows rolled down. There was no air conditioning and the outside temperature held at a steady ninety-six degrees. No one else was around. I positioned my head out of one of the windows. The first scent to hit me was buttered popcorn.

"What's that smell?" I asked.

My guide smiled wide, revealing strikingly white teeth against the backdrop of his dark skin.

He laughed, "Leopard pee."

"Leopard pee? No joke?"

"No joke."

But the overpowering smell was a pleasant lemon grass. The driver slowed.

"There. There over there, you go now."

My guide pointed to a majestic lion laying on top of some rocks. The jeep jerked forward as the driver tried to come to a silent smooth halt.

I slowly exited the jeep, leaving my door open. Adrenaline immediately hit and I began to shake. I was jittery and became concerned I wouldn't be able to make the shot. It was a male. The beast rested with its two paws in front of it. He looked like a house cat without a care in the world. Then, we locked eyes. I raised the .375 bolt action rifle provided by my guide. It was much more powerful than the rifle I typically used to hunt deer and expected a big kick and recoil. The lion realized something was wrong and stood to let out a roar. He started to walk toward me.

"Shoot! Shoot!" the guide cried from the safety inside the jeep.

As my finger touched the trigger, I was again transferred into the lion.

Nooooo, he thought. He somehow knew he would not survive our encounter. He had seen enough men hunting in these fields to know the result. It was becoming more difficult to fend off younger lions trying to take control of the pride and knew he was in the twilight of his life. But he figured he had more time. *Who will protect the others when I'm gone? Why do they hurt us?*

Animal Killer

The shot fired. The pain stung and the entry wound buzzed. At the time, I thought his death was more precise. I aimed for the heart, but experiencing it myself, I learned death was far from instant. The shot only tore part of the heart. The real and painful damage came from the bullet slicing through several organs and exploding the liver. Tormenting pain emanated from my belly. Bile poured into my blood stream and the result was a foul taste in my mouth. I fell to my side, stirring up the dry dirt into a puff of smoke. *Why? What did I do? Why did you do this to me?* He thought. Unconsciousness came quick and my eyes slowly closed as I watched myself grinning and examining the rifle. Darkness.

I woke up in a forest in Pennsylvania. Winter was days away. I remembered this too without the scene by scene replay. One of my more competitive coworkers was with me. We always tried to bigger and better one another. I listened to him brag for a solid two weeks about snagging a bear, which now lay spread on his floor in his home office. I couldn't take it anymore and was on the prowl for one of my own. A large black bear presented herself to me and I smiled as I pulled the trigger.

Once again, as I fired, I became the bear. I heard the shot first and then saw the smoke from the rifle. The bullet pierced a lung. As the bear, I charged toward myself when the second shot hit. In an instant, I felt my heart tear and explode inside my chest. I hit the ground hard, scattering the leaves. I reached with one paw, grasping inexplicably toward the tree line. Life quickly faded, but it didn't end before a collage of frantic thoughts. *Where are they? How are they going to survive? Is he going to kill them too? Please run.* My perspective then changed. I was pulled up to the sky, but stopped at the tree line. Less than fifty yards away I saw two cubs heading in my direction. The place where their dead mother lie. I understood their thoughts. They were in search for their mother and were starving. The mother I had just taken from them. I did not know that at the time. But now, I watched as I dragged their mother away. The cubs watching from a distance. Had I known they were there at the time, I would have most assuredly taken them too.

I recalled, that the following day I posted the picture of me and the dead bear carcass online for the world to see. My large, unrestrained, grin beside the bullet riddled bear with blood dripping from her mouth. The hostile comments began to roll in including from the kook, Sandy the bitch. The one who set me on the killing spree that led to my own death. This was the start of our war. I thought about my response, telling her that I intended to go kill more animals in her honor. It would be the following week my son and I killed two more. I posted the picture of my son and I and the fresh carcasses with the caption, that we had done it just for her and that we named one of them Sandy. This time, I imagined her pain. I visualized her in her home crying. The scene dissolved and the dark returned.

Without pause, more images chronicling every thing, big and small, that I had ever slaughtered, wounded or discarded played out as if they were as real as anything I had ever experienced. I endured all of the accompanying sensations. I lived all of the sights, sounds, smells and pain. I internally pleaded for these visions to stop, but they would not. I was at Karma's mercy.

Finally, the deer I slaughtered, just before I had been cut down by my son's stray bullet. I became the deer. I was battling with the doe beneath the tree where my rifle steadied and aimed right for it. He was searching for a mate and hoped he had just deemed himself worthy. But the shot, my shot, hit and that ended any hope of that. I took off in agony. The bullet entered near, but missed my heart, and then traversed through my lungs, lodging itself in the bone that attached my hind leg to my torso. I ran trying to get back to the herd. I wanted to see my friends again. Adrenaline coursing through me kept me going, but it was becoming more and more difficult to breathe. He wondered, *Why did this happen? What had I done?* I heard all of his thoughts and felt all he felt. The pain was immense. Life flowed out of me, leaving me numb and chilled. I could hear footsteps coming, but was unable to get up to flee. I looked into my eyes. I listened to me shout to the heavens, *"Who's the man!"* I watched in complete terror as the rifle aimed at my chest. I thought, *please no. Please help.* With the crack of the shot, all went dark, my life, its life, our life, ended.

The Eighth Chapter

I was back in the arena seated before the Deciders. My heart pounded so violently, I heard its thump against my chest. Some of the Deciders openly wept. Saint Francis' face was raging red. Karma remained stone cold. If I knew nothing else, I knew it was never a good sign when your judge or jury members wept after reviewing the evidence against you.

The crowd noise had reduced to a hush. I wondered if they had all just witnessed the killings and mayhem as I had. I assumed so, given the sudden somber atmosphere that palpably weighed on the Deciders. The masses began to rebound and recover from their shock. Their anger swelled.

"Murderer!" A shout cried in the distance.

"You're a sadist." Cried another.

I listened to the spectators shout obscenities and horrible charges against me. I turned to Karma.

"You talk about love. This is not love. What about all the good things I did? What about all I did for my family, and friends, and clients? All my hard work? All that means nothing? This is grossly unfair."

"Even after you saw all the damage and carnage you caused, you stiffen your resolve. You felt it, what it was like to be them. Yet, you still insist you are good. Worthy. You continue to defend your beliefs. The moral relativism under which you lived your life means nothing here. Or to me. A man spends his life giving to charity and doing good works, but murders his brother for his share of his father's inheritance. Is this a good man or a bad man? Is the sin of murder forgiven by all of his other kind acts? A sin, is a sin, independent of all other things. But set these things aside. Sins can be forgiven, if the wrongdoer repents. Sincerely repents. Repentance is not a word. It is a change of heart. Without it, the sin stands. Without it, you remain the sinner. This is the problem for you, because it appears this is what continues to rule your heart."

He said this without a hint of anger or pleasure. But with continued indifference.

"Fine. I am sorry. I won't kill animals if you say it is wrong. I promise."

I sounded like a spiteful child, apologizing for an offense he did not believe was wrong, and was doing so only after having been caught and chastised.

"Louie, there's no bargaining. You can't wrangle or lawyer your way out from judgment by offering the words you think we want to hear. What was done is done. The decision though is not up to any one of us. The Deciders will adjudicate these questions. The scale of Solomon will reveal your judgment."

"Please– just– wait one minute." Breathing became difficult over the panic. "You've got to give me a chance. Please."

Ignoring my plea, the Deciders rose and formed a circle to deliberate. The animal masses resumed the mantra, "*Justitia. Justitia. Justitia.*" I could not hear the Deciders over the noise. Karma moved to the Statue of Solomon and waited. Saint Francis stood facing the Deciders. His face still flush and red as he trembled. He would not be denied what he came for. He had the unwavering support of millions of angry creatures waiting for the verdict, held back weakly and possibly only temporarily by the swaying fence. They were ready to pounce and riot if they disapproved the outcome. Then, one by one, the ten Deciders each stepped forward and made their way to Karma. One by one they removed two glass spheres, each slightly larger than the size of a softball, from their robes and handed them to him. One red sphere, and one green.

Karma turned to me and explained.

"The red represents all of the unrighteousness and imperfections of your spirit. All the bad karma you have sowed. All the destruction you caused. All your ignorance and arrogance. The green represents all the love, and good, and mercy and kindness contained in your soul."

As each handed Karma a sphere, he would place the red ones on the left side of the scale, and the green on the right. As he did, the scale's pans seesawed up and down. With each movement, my anxiety waxed and waned. It appeared, even though every sphere was exactly the same size, their weights differed. The scale would tilt down or up as each were placed in the pans.

Love was the last to vote. The green sphere first. It contained all the joy, love and peace that embodied me. Love looked at me and smiled with contentment, pride and wonder. When Karma placed it on the cosmic scale, it tilted decidedly down, and to the right with the other green spheres. Love continued smiling at me. I repaid the gesture, smiling warmly to her. She abruptly turned away and handed Karma her red sphere containing all the hate, evil, darkness and suffering I caused. When he placed it on the other side, all she could do was weep, her face wet with tears. The scale, unquestionably, charged down and to the left. I didn't know what exactly that meant, but her reaction told the tale. She could no longer look at me. With the exception of Karma and Saint Francis, none of the Deciders looked at me. Their deliberations complete, and the verdict in, Karma moved to me.

"This is who you are, when the varnish of what you've covered yourself with is stripped away. Do not curse us because we peel away the facade, the false and ignorant beliefs you acquired. Do not be angered with us for revealing the whole truth. You're a nice guy. It's true. A decent family man, but, Louie, you fall short from the perfection of spirit expected and required to move on. You are love, and yet, you still did these horrible things. The many deer you slaughtered, animals you killed with your car, cats you injured, dogs you kicked, animals you turned your back on. These are not expressions of love. They are not expressions of worthiness. Balance must be restored and justice achieved. This is not about anger or revenge. You wounded these souls, the soul of God. It must be healed. The world you know and don't know needs to be healed. We heal through my works. You owe a debt to these animal souls. You owe a debt to God."

"I didn't do anything wrong!" I insisted.

I again heard a law school professor whispering in my ear, *"Deny, deny, deny!"* He would say, *"Always leave them with doubt."*

"Enough! It has been decided. You can agree to end this now and head to Oblivion. It can all be over. You will be no more. Or, you can accept the consequences of your conduct. Accept what justice demands."

"This is no choice. This is unfair," I said, looking at their faces, trying to catch a hint of reason in their eyes.

"This is the very definition of fair. You have seen what you've done. These are offenses against God. If you didn't know it before, you know it now. You will either continue to reject Him, or become the person you were meant to be. Be grateful you have the choice."

"Fine. I accept what your justice requires."

It wasn't really a choice at all.

"Take pause," he said. "Accepting the full force of justice due to you will not be easy. It will likely necessitate great suffering. It is the only way to achieve balance and give to you the opportunity to demonstrate the perfection of spirit God demands. Take heed, and proceed with caution, you may end up banished in Oblivion regardless."

Animal Killer

"Please– don't do this. I have suffered enough. As it is, I will never get to see my family again. Why? Tell me why does it have to be like this? How is this love? Doesn't God love?"

Saint Francis slammed his hand against the wood railing encircling his seat. Karma was startled by the interruption.

"Enough of his whining! Love has nothing to do with this," he shouted. "This is about justice. I say again, *Fiat justitia, ruat caelum*– let justice be done, even though the heavens fall!"

There was no negotiating. Karma returned his gaze to me, waiting for my answer.

"I accept." I said through clenched teeth.

Karma turned to the spectators and boomed, "He chooses to accept your justice."

The throngs exploded in glee. The chant of *"Justitia. Justitia. Justitia,"* resumed.

I was finished fighting. For me, Oblivion was no choice at all. One by one the Deciders came forward and hugged me. When Love embraced me, I felt the warmth, but she couldn't look me in the eyes. Each wished me luck. Each told me one way or another we would likely see one another, at least one more time.

The Teacher embraced me last. She whispered in my ear.

"Be sure to endure. Do God's will. Remember Jesus' response to the question asked by the lawyer, *'Who is my neighbor?'* That is the key–"

"I don't understand. I don't remember–" I tried to interrupt, but she continued,

"Do not allow your circumstances to dictate the man you are. If you remember what you've experienced and been taught here, you may have a chance to save yourself. That is what we all want for you. It will be the hardest thing you will ever do, to change. But if you truly want to save your soul, then there is no other way. Now go. Godspeed."

Part 2

Do not avenge yourselves, dear friends, but give place to God's wrath, for it is written, 'Vengeance is mine, I will repay,' says the Lord.

–Romans 12:19 NET

B. Lee Baker

The Ninth Chapter

With the decision made, Karma led me off the platform. We headed back toward the door from which we had entered. The Deciders remained behind. I shot one last look at the group in an unspoken feeble plea for them to change their mind, to spare me, but all of them, even Saint Francis, sadly watched without a further word as I departed. There would be no reprieve for me. I had no idea what came next. Fear gripped my bones, my knees buckled, making it difficult to move. *What would their justice look like? Feel like?* I trembled uncontrollably. As I neared the exit, the animals again, without concern for their individual well-being, hurled themselves against the containment fence. The flimsy barrier was all that kept them from tearing me apart. As I neared the exit, I felt like an athlete walking off the field after giving up the go ahead run. The fair-weather fans shouting down at him, *"You're a bum. Where did you learn to pitch? You suck!"* Only these spectators, the animals, shouted at me much worse.

"I am coming for you, Louie."

"You're dead man."

"Tables are turned now, dirt bag!"

I kept my head down and did not look any of them in the eye. The door opened. It no longer led to the tunnel and grand hallway where I had first arrived. Instead, it led into a colossal canyon. I became immobile. I wanted to run. I wanted out of this hell. I was tired of being judged. Karma grabbed my elbow.

"You go alone, armed only with your memories of a life spent killing, and with what you have learned here. I hope we will meet again. Accept God's will. Do not resist."

"I accept, I'm not resisting. Please— I ask again, stop this!"

"Time for you to go."

His voiced reduced to more of a whisper, revealing for the first time the faintest hint of something. I wouldn't call it emotion, maybe just the slimmest glimmer of concern.

"They're coming for you, Louie. Every one of them. They are coming for their justice. Use what you've learned. Now go, and be the Animal Killer no more."

"*Waaaait!* What do you mean they are coming for *me*? Who is coming? Learned, I didn't learn anything!"

"Then I fear there is no hope. Now, it's time. Run, Louie . . . run."

He let go of my arm and shoved me, shooting me through the door which closed immediately behind me and then disappeared. I closed my eyes and prayed, my body shaking with dread.

When I opened my eyes, I was no longer in the coliseum and what I saw before me was impossible. No longer restricted by the limitations of the human earthly body, I could see farther and perceive more. Although my body was the same, it was somehow different in some unexplainable way. The laws of the physical world seemed to still mostly apply, and yet, I found myself suspended above the beginning of a great canyon so large it had to be the size of the Earth itself. Then, I locked eyes with a black bear several miles away who returned my gaze with a dead stare. The bear raised a ram's horn to its mouth and blew out a shattering sound. The world shook and the face of the sky above the middle of the canyon cracked in half like an egg. The sky's perfectly uniform rich navy coloring transformed to a lighter blue with a crimson hue. The fissure created a rumbling, rolling thunder that did not relent. The bright white light outlining the tear had the brilliance and intensity of a lightning strike. From the tear, outpoured the animal and insect souls falling from Heaven, or some other place I did not want to contemplate. Every kind of species and sentient being to have ever lived or will ever live descended and joined the already populated canyon.

The bear continued to blast the horn in rapid intervals as these beasts fell from the gash in the world. Rather than falling to their deaths, each gently reached the ground below. They didn't wander, fight with one another or flee. Instead, they formed military-like columns. There were millions, billions, of them. Although I was unable to move, I had the ability to alter my vantage point and was able to perceive them from above and below, behind and in front. The deer led the charge. The cats, dogs, bears, pigs, chickens, squirrels and birds followed them. This animal army went on and on with apes, gorillas, monkeys, tigers, and lions. They all cried out, howling, chirping, cackling, roaring and screaming. The sound was horrifying. My eyes then caught, in sickening repulsion, the sight of humans being chased, trampled and feasted upon by lions, dogs, elephants and every other creature. The blood filled parts of the canyon one inch deep. With no warning, I dropped to the ground with a thud and expected death, whatever form that took in this place. Death did not come. Instead, the infinite animal horde began to march with military precision toward me. With each step they took, the ground rumbled. It felt and sounded like the fist of God pounding the Earth.

The animal army broke out with the now familiar cadence, *"Justitia. Justitia. Justitia."*

Justice would not be denied. Agony and terror strangled me. They were coming for me.

The air was still, but I was bone cold and chilled to the core. Terror-stricken and paralyzed, I did not move. The horn blaring in the distance was so deafening my teeth rattled. I thought the universe would break. The ground shook with increasing ferocity, sending shockwaves of nausea through me. I looked up and saw the gash in the sky repair itself. I thought of Karma's words, *"Run, Louie, run."* The hair on the back of my neck straightened and tingled, my testicles recoiled in fear. I had been stripped to my bare essentials. The camouflage hunting uniform I had been wearing at the time of my death was now gone. The thought of that outfit sent an unfamiliar wave of embarrassment washing over me that I could not reconcile, but, practically, the covering would have been immensely helpful. I was mercifully left wearing long underwear, but without any foot covering. In addition to the raw, piercing cold, oppressing thirst and hunger increased with each passing moment. I rubbed my dry tongue against the roof of my mouth, trying to generate saliva, but none came. My stomach growled in defiance. The feeling was stark and debilitating. *What was this place?* Two things were certain. This was definitely not Earth and the end of my prior life persisted. Karma's words again repeated in my mind, *"Then I fear there is no hope. . . . Run, Louie, run."* I shivered and knew I better conquer my paralysis and start moving.

The skills necessary to successfully hunt and those needed to survive are quite different, but thankfully there is some overlap. My mind was still reeling from the events from my death to this moment. I could not track time. There was too much to process. I, however, needed to set these thoughts aside. The time for reflection would come. For now, I needed to find some shelter and get some foot covering or I wasn't going to last long. Far-off in the distance I could make out a tree line. The beginning of a forest. Behind me was the canyon wall. Up was not an option. The sides of the valley were too flat and smooth, not to mention the staggering height. And, even if I could scale it, I had no idea where that would lead. The canyon itself was enormous. As far as I could see, in all directions, even beyond the forest, the canyon walls rose to touch the cracked sky. I was in a prison formed by the terrain. The horns precipitously quieted and the thunder of the progressing army halted.

Exhaustion crept in to join forces with the extreme cold, hunger, and thirst; each an unwelcoming expression of this terrifying world. I had too many priorities to address them all at once. So I chose evading capture to start, and headed to the tree line that was in the opposite direction from where I last heard thundering advancing army. The rocks littering the landscape and jagged ground cut at my feet. I scanned the countryside for something that would relieve the pain and stop the bleeding. While it was painful, the sting I experienced was different in an odd and fundamental way, but I had no time to analyze it. When I reached the tree line, I hesitated.

"Is anyone out there?" I called.

I waited for a response and scanned for any sign of life. Nothing but silence returned. I decided to proceed and weaved my way through the trees. The terrain turned more unforgiving on my bare feet. Blood seeped from the resulting wounds, leaving behind a crimson trail. Finally, I found what I had been looking for, a group of birch trees. Amazed, I remembered many years ago I read a survival article in a monthly hunters' magazine about how you could make shoes from the bark of white birch trees. I found a sharp rock and scraped at the bark. I managed to cut and peel long flat vertical strips from the tree's circumference. I then laid the strips down and crisscrossed them weaving them together so it looked like a tic-tac-toe board or basket weave. I then stepped on them and tied them up around my ankles. They would not last, but they offered relief. I sat with my back against the tree and contemplated my next move. I needed clean water, food and shelter.

A vibrating rumble broke the silence and my disjointed assessment of my plight. The ground resumed quaking. The marching army pushed on, moving in my direction. They must have picked up my scent and were now coming fast. I stood and looked around. *Run, Louie, run*, my mind screamed. There was no place to hide. I had no idea where I was going or what would happen if the animal army caught up to me. I didn't want to find out. I needed to defend myself. I snapped off a branch from a tree that was the perfect size to use as a weapon, if needed. I hoped it wouldn't come to that. I took off running with the primitive weapon in tow. I paused momentarily and looked up to the alien sky which revealed nothing.

"What do you want from me?" I cried.

Animal Killer

I continued to move while silently praying. My stomach rejected the prayer, growling with hunger in response. My lips and tongue continued to dry and became cracked and coarse. I headed deeper into the darkening woods, stalked by the gaining army. An inconceivable army that included countless apex predators, rodents, insects, and everything in between. *How was any of this possible? What did they want from me? Justice? What did that mean? What would it look like? Did they want me dead?* I was already gone. I ran for as long as I could. Every few feet I thought I heard branches break and feared I was being surrounded.

And then, as fast as the army started, they sharply stopped. The forest grew still and quiet and I stopped to catch my breath. I hoped I lost them. My chest heaved and perspiration bathed me.

"*Screetch . . . Ekkk,*" the silence exploded from above without warning.

A screaming cacophony of countless turkey vultures, falcons and hawks numbering in the thousands, maybe more, flew above me. They blotted out the sky. Every other species of bird trailed behind them. The collective tone was of such a deafening pitch it reminded me of the fire alarm in my office building. The sound was earsplitting and penetrated into my brain so violently it vibrated my skull and bones. The pain was excruciating. I had to get away. I dropped the stick and ran with my hands over my ears. Panic and pain exchanged places within me as the mixed flock chased after me.

The turkey vultures with their fat black bodies that looked too large to fly, red heads, pale steel-like beaks and six foot wing spans, dove and snapped at my head, back and hands, tearing and splitting my flesh. They were menacing creatures who typically fed on road kill. In my case, they made an exception, feasting on me while I ran. My ears began to adjust to the paralyzing sound, but they still rang and throbbed. I grabbed another branch, but each time I stopped running, the siren rained down the unbearable upon me. I swung the branch wildly– desperate to knock them from the sky. Every so often I got lucky, connecting with one dive-bombing at me, causing it to collide with a tree or the ground. Up ahead the forest grew thicker and provided cover. There were so many birds the air *whooshed* and *whipped* about.

Deeper in the forest, I freed myself from the squeals of the birds and roar of the advancing army. I caught the sound of gushing water and immediately headed toward it. Mercifully, I located the source quickly. It was a full blown rapid river. I knelt down and carefully reached my hands in to taste its coolness as it rushed by. I decided it was fresh and took my chances. I furiously cupped the cold water in my hands and brought it to my mouth. After a few unsatisfying attempts, I plunged my head below the surface and gulped. I started to choke, and even though I remained thirsty, I came up for air. Fits of coughing expelled much of the cold water that lodged itself deep within my lungs. Wet, I was now even colder. I was so exhausted that I sat beside the river for a moment to catch my breath. I closed my eyes and allowed the water to stream down my face. I did not hear anything other than the rapids from the river rushing passed me and smashing against rocks. It was my first moment of peace since I met Karma. When I opened my eyes I was surrounded. Looking down at me was an oversized deer, a black bear and a golden lion.

I jumped to my feet letting out an involuntary, *"Whooohh!"*

The animals surprisingly didn't flinch from my sudden movement. Most deer will flee in fear at the slightest activity. Behind the three, as far as I could see, stood countless creatures of every kind. They appeared to be a rabid army of more deer, bear, elephants, hyena, squirrels, cats, dogs, cows, chickens, turkeys, fish, hippos, insects of every species, including bees. I always hated bees more than anything. They apparently didn't like me either, having stung me several times over the course of my life. *Ughh, of all things, why bees?* The enormous brown deer in the lead stepped forward. I was speechless. As he drew closer I could discern that he was an Irish elk. I knew it was an Irish elk and learned that they had gone extinct because I had seen one, a replica in a lodge my father took me to when I was a boy. He stood before me, ferociously menacing, seven foot tall at the shoulder. He probably weighed sixteen hundred pounds. His antlers were so large they wouldn't fit through a barn door. He was a magnificent animal. My first thought was that his head would have looked perfect in my office, but quickly realized the room was not nearly large enough to hold this beast. He was flawless. An unblemished brown pelt, well defined muscles that looked like they would power him to run for days. And then, as if it had always been so, and perfectly natural, he began to speak.

"Well . . . as I live and breathe, why– *ain't* it the famous Animal Killer right here in our little neighborhood. Welcome to Damnation, Louie." He spoke deliberately, with a southern twang. "We've been *waitin* on you big man. You here to give us a little justice? Karma good enough to send you our way? Allow us a little . . . retribution?" He mocked.

Animal Killer

After an awkward pause, he continued.

"Oh, where are my manners. We must have a proper introduction. You can call me, Azrael. I'm top *dawg* in these parts, so to speak. If you were *wonderin*, Karma don't have no say *'round* here. Neither do them Deciders. You see, in this place, we get to decide what happens to you."

He smiled, turning to the creatures behind him, they looked eager to tear me apart.

"These are the offended. Your victims. Their families and their friends. Remember your victims? He again paused, studying me. "Why do you look so puzzled and confused? You know, your conquests, the ones you slaughtered and maimed just for a little fun. A little ego boost. I hope you don't consider it rude of us to demand a little justice."

"This is not real." I blurted aloud.

"Oh, this is very real, *Louieee.*" He said my name mockingly.

"How do you know my name? What– What do you want from me? What's going to happen?"

I felt small and helpless. A far cry from the days when I had commanded a courtroom.

"Oh, we know all about you, *Louieee.* What'd you think is *gonna* happen? They told you there would be justice and consequences. Suffering. Now, did you honestly think you could slaughter us and expect no retribution? You called us animal, with disdain, like it's a four letter word. You mocked us. But our time for vengeance is now. Where I come from, when a man mass murders like you, we make certain he receives his comeuppance. All day long. That real enough for you? Time to learn firsthand the suffering you inflicted. Time for you to learn how it feels. It's time for justice to be done. You've taken our sons and daughters, mothers and fathers, brothers and sisters. Taken our friends. You did it for no good reason other than to boost your false sense of worth and power. You did it . . . to be *cooool*. You did it because you could, because you believe yourself to be superior. And, when you weren't going out of your way to massacre us, you were just plain cruel and indifferent. And, then you walked into that pretty church and claimed to be a good Christian boy. A man of God."

"What do you want from me? I didn't do anything wrong. This has nothing to do with religion. You're just a bunch of animals and bugs. I was a good person. Good to people." I rebuked, trying to hide my ever-increasing panic.

I stated this with my lifelong conviction of its truth. But, as I said it, the words didn't taste right in my mouth as I faced those who suffered. Like telling a lie, it tastes a little bit different than the truth. The words tugged and gnawed as I said them, they came out twisted, untrue.

Azrael turned to the gathering army behind him, "Can you believe this guy? He still don't get it. Why'd they even give him a chance? Poor *Louieee* was a good person. Doesn't know what he did wrong." He turned back to me. "Okay, *Louieee*, have it your way. We're just a bunch of animals. We don't matter. We're *gonna* give you your wish and act accordingly. We'll show you what it is like to be without power, outnumbered, and out gunned. You took our lives, how about we take your soul? How does that sound? Sound about right with you?" He said, glaring at me with dark angry, dead eyes.

I couldn't accept what was happening. I knew retribution would come my way, but I thought the Deciders gave me another chance. Another life. A last try. I could not accept this was God's will. It seemed so absurd that this was how He rendered judgment. How could this beast take my soul? I was an experienced hunter. What could a bunch of animals do? But then again, animals are not supposed to be able to talk and work together as these were. I had no weapon or any idea how to fight this army alone. It was all very difficult to process. I wished this had been a bad dream. But it wasn't. I was staring reality in the face. And, it stared right back at me in the form of a seven foot, sixteen hundred pound, extinct, talking Irish elk. Azrael took a step toward me. Adrenaline and instinct kicked in, I could think of nothing else except to jump into the river and ride the current. I wasn't going down without a fight.

I jumped in. The moment I touched the water, the raging river swept me away. The animal army, now behind me on land, erupted. I was exceedingly proud of myself for my quick thinking and reaction. My confidence and victory was short lived. Hundreds of fish that inexplicably joined the army on land leapt into the water after me. A sonic boom exploded as the turkey vultures and accompanying birds took off to the sky after me. The ground reverberated as the rest followed on land. I was again being chased. But my most immediate concern was the river itself. It was a violent ride. It tossed me around without effort. I had difficulty keeping my head above the water, a constant drag pulled me below the surface. I tried not to panic, but was finding it difficult to breathe. I kept going under, swallowing sickening amounts of the frigid water. It was like being on a rollercoaster moving up and down with the terrain below. I became sick. The cold water was so extreme a hypothermic paralysis began to grip me. My heart raced. The swarm of birds became so thick they darkened the sky above. There had to be millions of them. I didn't know how I would escape. But first, I had to free myself from the force of the current and exit the river. My lungs burned and ears began to buzz. Blue and white lights twinkled about the corners of my eyes. I thought I would drown and squander the chance the Deciders offered me. I tried to time taking my breaths when I was above the water line, but it proved impossible as the river swept me along. I accepted that if I drowned, at least this nightmare would be over.

The canyon walls closed in and confined the river on both sides making it feel like an Olympic luge with its many kinks and curls. There was nowhere for me to go. I was at the mercy of the ride. I was moving so fast and quickly accelerating, the turkey vultures and the other flying fowls lagged behind, unable to keep up as I pulled away. Finally, the enclosed canyon thankfully ended and opened up, presenting some hope I could pull myself out of the water.

The water carried me at breakneck speed, concealing any warning of the raging soaring waterfall ahead. It was too late to do anything once I saw it. I had no way to stop myself. Nothing to grab. It happened so fast. I shot over the edge, only then seeing just how high this fall was going to be. This was it. It was the end.

I was airborne for what felt like an eternity. I expected everything to go dark when I hit the surface below. I straightened my body and tensed every muscle before the impact. The smack of the water burned my skin and blew out all the air I had temporarily borrowed. I cut the surface and was pushed deep under the water. I needed to get air fast and rocketed back toward the surface. When I broke free from the grip of the water, my lungs immediately clutched for the available air. With the fall behind me, the current slowed, allowing me to swim over to land and pull myself out of the river. I was exhausted and shivering, but I forced myself to push on, crawling, I made my way under some trees to hide from the turkey vultures and their fellow fighters that no doubt continued to pursue me. I stumbled upon a pile of leaves and tumbled in. I pulled the heap on top of me for warmth and cover and collapsed.

I don't know how long I was out before the sounds of horns woke me. I exploded up and out from the leaves, not knowing where I was. Then, the punch of reality hit me once again. The thunder of the murderous army roared, announcing they were closing in. I had to move fast. I got up and ran away from what I thought was the direction of the sound of the marching army. I needed new foot covering and also needed to sleep. I needed food, and surprisingly, my thirst persisted. It seemed no matter how much I drank, I could not quench my thirst. I needed a break to figure out what I was going to do. Maybe, more importantly, I needed to figure out what I was supposed to do.

As I moved onward, every few feet, I glanced over my shoulder and up to the sky, a decision nearly fatal. I wanted to make sure no thing was close behind me, but should have been focused on what lie before me. I spun around when my feet slipped, almost falling off the side of a cliff. I was barely able to stop my momentum before careening over the side, into a deeper valley below. It was the valley I had seen earlier from a distance. It was filed with hundreds, thousands, of men and women, disemboweled, lying atop of one another, but all still alive and slowly crawling and moving. They were bathed in blood, several inches deep. I quickly turned, desperate to get away from this place.

I moved through the trees and up and down the terrain for what may have been hours or minutes. I couldn't tell. I eventually came to a clearing. Rising from below the ground was a titanic wooden wall. The logs were made from unearthly giant oak trees strung together. The top of each log was carved to the finest deadly point. The wall wrapped the landscape for miles. I didn't know if this fortress was meant to hold something in, or keep others out.

Then I spotted two bronze doors carved into the wall. Inscribed into the door on the left read, "*Spiritus.*" The door on the right read, "*Exterminatore.*" My heart sank. Karma had made a mistake, or the Deciders had changed their minds. Either way, it seemed I was sent to the Spirit Destroyer. This was his realm, and these animals, his minions. I was in Damnation. If that realization was not depressing enough, when I turned my gaze from the doors, I spotted two men nailed to thick wooden tree trunk sized posts sunken deep into the ground. It was a crucifixion. Instead of the classic *T* shape crucifix, they were spread out in an *X* shape with their arms pinned over their heads and away from their bodies. Their legs spread far apart, barely touching the ground. There were hundreds of these *X*-styled crucifixion stations lining the front of the wall hiding the Spirit Destroyer. I became nauseous and wept. I knew I had to remain quiet or risk being caught. I put my hands to my face to muffle my cries.

The Tenth Chapter

I had never been squeamish and have witnessed some gruesome sights hunting, but the spectacle of the crucifixions sickened me. After a moment, the shock dissipated and I calmed myself. I moved closer to get a better look. I looked at all those empty crucifixion stations and pushed away the thoughts that wanted to come with that. My heart seized and fluttered when I got closer and saw what should have been impossible. The two men were alive, but they were disemboweled. Three dogs were eating one of the men. Two pit bulls and a German shepherd. They were large and angry. The dogs' fur around their mouths and snouts were stained with blood. The frenzy caused an over-production of their saliva, the excess dripping from their mouths. It also sprayed in every direction as they twisted their heads going in for another bite and tearing at the flesh. My mind cried, *that's going to be you if you get caught!* Neither man should have been alive. Their chests were open and I could see their hearts beating. I moved even closer, careful to remain concealed. There was so much blood I was hit with the taste of metal in my mouth. The iron from the blood flooded the air, landing on my tongue, creating the similar sensation when biting aluminum foil. I shuddered. The man being attacked pleaded with the dogs.

"Please. Listen to me. I am sorry. Please, figure out how to just kill me. Oblivion. I beg you. End this. How much longer will this last?" He cried.

The dogs laughed. I never heard a dog laugh before. To say it was creepy is an understatement. I had made a bad decision coming to this place. If it was really my decision at all.

One of the dogs responded.

"You should have thought about that before you decided to force us to fight one another in your backyard, for money. You should have thought about that before you butchered us!" The dog screamed. "Maybe you should have considered the consequences of drowning us when we couldn't or wouldn't fight each other. And, don't you lie. Don't you tell me you're sorry when you're not! You're sorry for where you are now. You're not sorry for what you did!" The pit bull growled and continued to bite and chew at the man.

Animal Killer

I didn't notice it at first, but there were wooden signs affixed above the two men. The signs extended across the top of the crucifix with each side nailed into the top of the left and right side. The one above the pleading man had "Sadistic Abuser" carved into it. The other simply read, "Sport Hunter." There were two large hairy black apes and a monstrous black bear nailing a sign to the wooden cross post next to the Sport Hunter. Without warning, the black bear dropped the sign he had been holding and spun around in my direction. His eyes narrowed and his brown and black snout perched into the air. He began to inhale with great determination, sniffing, his nostrils contracting. I was behind a tree and bushes and didn't think he could see me, but became alarmed he could smell me. I froze and held my breath. He remained fixated on my location. The two apes also turned, curious to see what caught the bear's attention.

After a moment, the bear gave up and the three resumed their construction. I feared moving until I knew for sure they lost interest. *How are these animals able to do these things?* I was challenged to comprehend, but I began to accept the new reality of this world and let go of my experiences and understandings from my former life. I had seen so much since my death, the inconceivable, no longer shocked me. So I thought.

The apes and the bear had the dexterity to hold a hammer and nail the sign to the crucifix. The apes also had crossbows and a quiver of arrows strapped across their backs. *Were they hunters?* I had to wait for them to finish and step away to read the sign they had just completed installing. It read, "Animal Killer."

My mind shouted, *run!* But fear regained its grip, paralyzing me. My legs felt heavy and stuck, refusing to move. A rolling thunder then roused me out of the terror induced state where I had receded. The rumble sounded like the sonic boom of military jets. It grew in its intensity as they came closer. It reminded me of being at a baseball stadium during the playoffs. Military jets would fly overhead before the start of the game. My teeth would vibrate and I couldn't hear anything above the boom.

When they reached me, the sky darkened and my bones rattled. It was the birds. There were even more of them this time. They flew unlike any bird flock I had ever seen. Instead of the migratory *V* shape I had seen so many times during my life, these birds flew the way an army marched on land. They flew in perfect rows and columns. An army of the air. Searching for me. I was being hunted by land, sea and air. As they sped by, the leaves on the trees rustled and branches swayed and cracked. Thankfully, the forest canopy covered me and I remained undetected.

I shook off the terror and decided to get far away from this place. I insisted this all had to be a cosmic misstep. Karma either sent me to the wrong place, or I mistakenly believed I would be sent back to Earth to receive some measure of reasonable retribution. I didn't contemplate any of this. I had to evade this animal army at all costs. Mistake or not, I suspected if captured, they would deliver me to the Spirit Destroyer who would feast on my soul as Karma promised. If this was a mistake, I had to survive just long enough to give Karma time to correct it.

Suddenly, the ground rumbled. I had to get away, so I ran. My makeshift foot covering loosened and I would need new ones soon. I needed a bed, some warm clothes and a meal. I needed to rest, but I could not have any of that right now. I had to keep moving. It was then I heard that sound again, that *"whoosh!"* I instantly knew that it was too late, the arrow pierced my calf. The excruciating pain was unlike any I had experienced. I could still run, but my leg, my calf, throbbed with every step.

Then a shout.

"There!"

I had been spotted.

I took off running, zig zagging around the trees. Arrows whizzed by my head. Many lodged themselves in the tree trunks around me. I was in an outright run, but the incline of the terrain and my cut, bark covered, feet made it difficult to move fast. I moved up and down with the topography. At the peak of the incline, I saw on the other side a meadow below the steep mountainside. There was no place to hide, but I couldn't turn back. I paused for a moment and snapped the back of the arrow embedded in my calf. I held my breath and pushed the remaining arrow forward forcing it through the front of my leg. Despite the gaping wound and spilling blood, I immediately felt better. I slid down the mountainside and ran through the meadow at the bottom. I turned back and saw the animals in pursuit. A pack of black bear were tracking and gaining on me fast. Hundreds of apes brought up their flank. Behind the apes, the deer, lions, tigers, hyena, horses, and other predators spread out, encircling me. Collectively, they were a wave of fury coming at me, as menacing and destructive as any human army of the Earth. I needed to get away to find cover.

"I am going to make it. I am going to make it." I rapidly repeated out loud, in between breaths as I sprinted ahead, tears streaming from the corners of my eyes.

My breathing became heavy and uneven, interrupted, and made more difficult, by the gasps caused by fear and the frantic chase. I ran until I could run no more. My lungs burned and my calf throbbed. I was physically and emotionally drained. I made it to the edge of another forest and staggered in. The air in the distance whipped about from patrolling birds above and the ground continued to shake. They were closing in. I looked around to decide where to go next when I realized I was in the midst of a sea of fallen leaves so thick they were piled as high as my knees. I quickly dove into them and buried myself. The smell, a mixture of dirt and pollen, overwhelmed me. I hoped the cover would be enough to hide me. I closed my eyes and tried to calm myself as I prayed silently.

God, please make this stop. I was a good man. I provided for my family. I took care of my friends. I was a good Catholic. I then prayed the Lord's Prayer. It seemed appropriate under the circumstances. I finished with an empathic, but silent, *Amen!* I hoped that would get the Big Man's attention and get Him to correct Karma's mistake.

I could not accept any of this was real. The charge God cared so much about animals was fantastic to me, and considered my lot in this life terribly unfair. I refused to believe that I was in this hell simply because I did a little hunting and had been mean to a few animals and insects. This had to be a mistake. I was sure of it. Karma's words, *They demand justice,* rang hollow. *This was not justice,* I silently retorted. This was disproportionate punishment for a crime I didn't know existed. *Ignorance of the law is no excuse,* I heard my first year criminal law professor instruct. Still, I had already lost my life. Lost my family. Punishment enough I countered. My thoughts involuntarily jumped to the killing scenes Karma forced me to relive. The pain and unhappiness of those animals and those around them, I had to admit, bothered me immensely. I forcibly dismissed those thoughts. I would not be manipulated.

My stubbornness notwithstanding, Karma and Saint Francis triggered a war within me that would not relent. I remained convinced I did nothing wrong, but given my current reality, I couldn't help but consider the truth of their charges. My internal debate halted the moment I heard the nearby leaves rustle and branches crack. The animals were just about on top of me. The ram's horn wailed every minute or so. I had no idea if it was their way of communicating or whether it was an announcement of their power and divinity meant to strike terror and fear in their prey. It reminded me of the drums and trumpets carried onto the battlefield during the American Revolution. The ground continued to tremble. As they got closer, the sensation and sound reminded me of being in a movie theater watching a World War II movie. The tanks rolling through some small French town would cause the theater to vibrate and shake, creating the life-like feeling you were there. Dogs began to bark and growl. They were so close I heard them pant. The marching stopped. I held my breath, but I continued to shake from the cold and fear.

Everything became still. There wasn't a sound. After what seemed like an eternity, the ground began to rumble again and the swarm continued on. I breathed again, relieved.

"Thank you, God." I said quietly.

Something also buried in the leaves with me then moved and brushed against my leg. I froze with fear. Then, a second thing moved and crawled onto my arm. A third set of feet made their way atop my stomach and started to move toward my face. I cursed myself for making a sound and suppressed the urge to get up and run. I brushed away some of the leaves to see what was crawling on me. Rats. My torso reflexively shot up. The cloak of the leaves falling, exposing me. I thought they had moved on, but a platoon of angry, deadly animals stood there surrounding me. A powerful massive ape moved quickly and was the first to reach me. He thrust his thick hairy arm into the pile still hiding half of me and grabbed me by my right ankle. He viciously yanked me out from the leaves with the rats clinging to me.

"Let me go!" I said, kicking and screaming.

No matter what I tried, I could not break free. The ape maintained his vice-like grip, tossing me around effortlessly. He then dragged me. The rocks scattered about on the ground smashed against my head causing immense pain and a blistering ringing in my ears. My flesh tore and my blood spilled. I thought I was going to surely die from the drag. Worse than the excruciating injuries and assault, was the fear that I knew where he was bringing me.

The animal army followed. They chanted in unison,

"Justitia. Justitia. Justitia."

I did not want to be crucified. Imagining the coming agony made me retch, but nothing came up. Any hope I was wrong ended when I spotted the crucifixion stations through the blood streaming down my face. The two men I had seen earlier remained enslaved and fixed to their crosses, the brown soil beneath them turned orange, stained with their blood. Earlier, their bodies had been split apart and dismantled, now, the men were physically undamaged. My new reality. One of the apes hoisted me up and threw me against my assigned crucifix. Struggling was useless. I was at their whim and mercy, of which there was none.

Azrael stepped out from the tree line surrounded by his army.

"Seems we got ourselves a runner. That's real good. We like a challenge."

Azrael's southern accent becoming a little more southern.

"It can get a little . . . monotonous 'round these parts. So we have to make it– interesting. You see, like you, Louie, we hunters too. And, we love *huntin* mother fuckers as much as you like *huntin* deer. And, you, Louie, you're real mother fucker. A real big man. *Ain't* that right? A real big man preying on the innocent. *Hiddin* in the trees and behind the bushes." He gyrated his head and body around to help illustrate and accentuate his point. "Crouching down real quiet like. Yeah, that's real brave, real tough." He stepped closer as if he were going to stomp me to death. "Cradling your little weapon someone else made for you. Cause, let's face it, you *ain't* good enough, or smart enough, to make it yourself. Wearing your ridiculous costume to help you hide so we can't see you. Making sure it *ain't* no fair fight. What *y'all* think?"

He asked the army behind him, but never turned his gaze from me.

"Sounds like something a real man would do, don't it?" He took another step closer to me. "Actually . . . sounds cowardly to me, like a scared little bitch. What *y'all* think, how would our boy here make out in a fair fight?"

This triggered uncontrollable laughter from the other animals. He had obviously done this before and knew how to give a good show. He turned back to me.

"What'd you think was *gonna* happen here, boy? Let me see if I can explain it to you. You see, the roles are, how'd you say, the roles are reversed. You see, in these parts, I am the head honcho. I am the angel of death and destruction in this place. I am the mother fucker. Oh, wait . . . let me put in terms *y'all* understand. Who's da man?"

My mind jumped to my conquest cry after tracking down and killing that deer right before my own death.

Not waiting for an answer, he repeated with scorn, "Who's *da* man?"

He moved even closer to me, I could feel his breath. We locked our eyes and he spoke slowly.

Animal Killer

"Let me tell you who's *da* man. Why . . . I'm *da* mother fucking man now, Louie. *Ain't* I? And once I got your ass, you *ain't* escaping."

And, then, in an instant, he turned and relaxed, breaking the tension.

"You should see my den. I got all you fools lined up on my wall. Your head is *gonna* look real nice stuffed and mounted there. I got a nice prime spot *waitin* just for you. I've been *waitin* on you for a real long time, *Louieee*. But we're *gonna* have a little fun first."

I refused to look at him any longer and stared at the ground. He tilted and dipped his head beneath mine so he could continue to look directly into my eyes.

"Cheer up, sport. You look so glum. I thought you like *huntin?* We *gonna* spend some time *huntin* together. It's *huntin* season. Only, you're *gonna* get to experience it on the other end. What's fair is fair, don't you think?"

He nodded and one ape began hammering steel spikes through my wrists while another ape drove two through my ankles, fixing me to my wooden crucifix below the sign that read, "Animal Killer."

I let out a wail. *"Noooooooo!"*

The anguish gripped my entire body, down to the bone. The first spike pierced an artery projecting blood across the ape's face, wetting and staining his black hair. My bones crunched and shattered. The sound reminded me of the snap from the wishbone we pulled apart at Thanksgiving. I kept waiting for unconsciousness to claim me. It never did. Instead, a new wave of nausea struck me and I began to sweat. The beads of perspiration collecting at my hairline streamed down my face. Some migrated into my eyes, stinging them and partially blinding me. I lost control and urinated down my leg, soaking my pants. The warmth that I welcomed initially turned into a curse when it cooled and created even more discomfort. The metal spikes piercing my wrists and legs caused unbearable physical pain. My mind unsuccessfully chased unconsciousness for relief from the torture, exhaustion and shock. I was pinned and prone, strung up like a slaughtered gutted deer. After several moments, the initial pain passed and I realized the hurt and suffering was not actually physical pain at all. My mind deceived me, having lived a life understanding what physical pain looks and feels like. The more accurate description of the sensation, instead, was an emotional, not a physical, pain. Each act of cruelty and each spike piercing me caused me to experience catastrophic emotional trauma. It produced the same psychological impacts caused by the horrific deaths of those I loved, a thousand betrayals, abandonment, beatings; every imaginable and unspeakable act of unconstrained brutality all compressed into the point of each spike. And yet, this did not begin to adequately chronicle what was being done to me. They were not traumas and damage to my flesh, they were lacerations and wounds to my soul. I was unsure if the damage was mortal, as Azrael had threatened. I was unsure if I would survive, or even if I wanted to. Every negative emotional thing that happens, or could ever happen, in one's lifetime concentrated into a single event, into a single point. That is what each of the spikes caused me. My life force faded, I began dying by degrees.

"Now, we're *gonna* have you hang out here for a bit. Pun intended. *Ya* see, we don't want no fair fight, Louie. Just like you, wouldn't be any fun if it's a fair fight and our necks were on the line. If we had . . . skin in the game. So we're *gonna* have you hang here and when we're ready to go *huntin* . . . we'll let *ya* down."

He lowered his voice so only I could hear him.

"But I'll let you in on a little secret. It's not us that should concern you the most. We're just the tenderizer. What should really twist you is what that Spirit Destroyer is going to do with you once we're done. He's *waitin* on you. Right there, just behind that wall. He's the one you should be *worryin* about. He's the main course. He'll do the real damage and be the one to end it. In the meantime, let's have some fun, sport."

I pleaded with him.

"Please. Please, let me go. I don't deserve this. I'm so cold and hungry."

"Don't waste your time," the Sport Hunter hanging next to me interrupted. "They don't care, and there is no way to make it stop until they feel like they have gotten their pound of flesh. Until they have gotten their vengeance," he said with a deranged smile.

Azrael shot the Sport Hunter a look.

"You sure you got something to say on this subject?"

The Sport Hunter went silent and immediately bowed his head.

I began to weep. Tears streamed down my cheeks mixing with the sweat and blood.

"You're a real peach, Louie. Let me ask, you ever give those animals you hunted a chance to rest? You ever give them a meal before you shot them dead? I don't think so. What are you *cryin 'bout*, boy? I thought you were a tough guy? Wasn't it a short time ago you was bragging about how big and bad you are? You always bag the biggest buck, *ain't* that right? Look at you now. Pathetic, sobbing just like the wretch you truly are," he spit.

Animal Killer

He then turned his back and disappeared into the forest.

I hung there, shivering, aching, and bleeding, unable to do anything except await my fate, which I knew, would get far worse.

B. Lee Baker

The Eleventh Chapter

The first attack came at night. I couldn't be sure, but I believe it was shortly after Azrael disappeared into the forest. It was the first time since I had arrived that dark descended upon this vengeful world. The lack of regular and consistent days contributed to my inability to mark the passage of time. It was unsettling and compounded the discomfort I felt. It came without a sound. It came without warning. I didn't even know it was happening until the assault was well under way. Thousands, maybe millions, of ants swarmed over me. They crept under my clothes and crawled all over my body. They made their way toward my head. I felt them burrowing into my belly button. They climbed into my nostrils and in my ears. I would swear I heard one of them say, "Time for retribution." I slammed my mouth shut and closed my eyes. I could feel them entering me. Several perched themselves on my eyebrows and lifted my eyelids open. They bit me and started to feed on my eyes. Inside, they began to feast on my brain and other organs. It was deliberately slow. Agony in its most naked form. I couldn't move, still pinned to my cross. The agonizing sensation was again not physical. The attack deepened the wounds that had already been inflicted upon my soul by the metal spikes. It worsened my dread and sense of loss and abandonment. I was drained. I opened my mouth to scream and plead for death, but they flooded inside and down my throat before I could let it out. After some time, I no longer cared about anyone or anything. Then, as quickly as it came, it ended. The ants retreated into the night. I was left as a skeleton. The way a dog picks a chicken bone clean down to the marrow. I wept. Again.

I moved in and out of consciousness for some unknowable time. When I regained my mind, I realized my body, ravaged by the ants, had somehow regenerated itself. As I cursed God for allowing this to happen to me, the second offensive started. I didn't see them at first. I could only hear them as the trees rustled. Then, in a sudden and violent explosive coordinated attack, they shot out from the tree line. This time it was squirrels. They sprinted at full speed, heading directly for me. I still couldn't move. There was nothing I could do to defend myself. They leapt onto me clawing and biting every part of me. They tore and chewed my flesh. I closed my eyes. They then chewed on my eyelids, consuming and digesting them, like the ants, forcing me to watch the onslaught. I opened my mouth to scream and one shot his head inside my mouth and started to chew my tongue. I tried to bite down to fight back, but other squirrels held my mouth open. They managed to chew through my stomach and spilled out my intestines. My insides dangled from my belly down to the floor. I cannot say how long the assault lasted. It felt like an eternity. And then suddenly, like the ants, they retreated and disappeared as quickly as they came. But the damage had been done. The attack further intensified my never-ending anguish. The damage to my soul worsened. I was being slowly destroyed from the inside out. There was nothing I could do to stop or slow it. There was no one to reason with. No way to bargain, no choice but to accept it for what it was. Sick revenge.

I became semi-catatonic. It was welcomed amnesty from the immense, unrelenting, suffering. Not nearly as desirable as sleep or unconsciousness, but a break nonetheless. My trance was not the result of the beatings and maiming, but rather stemmed from the crushing weight of despair being forced upon me. It was an involuntary defensive mechanism of my mind to help stave off the incomprehensible trauma. I wished I had the ability to will it. If I could, I would enter and remain there, never to return. Unfortunately, the sustained cruelty of this place pulled me out from my daze. My consolation, when I looked down, my body was unbroken. My eyelids restored, I was again able to shut my eyes, my entrails also returned to their rightful place. I thought maybe I had merely imagined the vicious encounters and mutilation I had surely suffered.

The third attack quickly disabused me of the notion that these events might be imaginary. It was entirely, and horrifically, real. I heard his breathing before I ever caught a glimpse of him. It escalated to grunts and progressed to growls. I could not locate him, only hear him. He was moving about from side to side. I was trying to twist my head to see behind me, but could only stretch my neck so far. When I turned my head back around, he stood before me. He puffed and snarled.

He moved closer to me. He was big. Four, maybe four and one half, feet tall at the shoulder. His head topped out at almost five feet. He tilted his head up so that his mouth was almost in front of my face, then he let out a deafening roar. His warm breath punched my face. Its force so powerful, my hair blew back. His coat, golden yellow-brown. His mane, well-groomed. His paws, exceptionally large and plump with razor-like retractable claws. His mouth, housing his teeth, was his most menacing feature that showcased two large fangs that seemed too long to fit inside. Drool smothered them as the slobber dripped from his chin to the ground below. He was so close I could see his teeth were stained yellow. There was not an ounce of fat on him, and like Azrael, his muscles were well pronounced on his muscular body. He was a killing machine. Mano a mano, he was on top of the food chain. His eyes, however, conveyed a profound sadness and anger at the same time. A pain that could never be healed. The rest of the world grew quiet. There was no sound other than the growls and heavy breathing coming from deep within the belly of the beast. The air was very still, but for his breath moving in and out hitting me in the face. He didn't move right away. He let the moment, the fear I was internalizing, marinate. He wanted to take his time. There was no rush.

The Sport Hunter still impaled next to me had been quiet since chastised by Azrael, but now broke his silence.

"I'm sorry, man. The good news is they can't, or won't kill you. But, the bad news is they can't, or won't kill you. At least not on their own. Not without taking you to that thing on the other side of the wall."

Four large apes sprung from the trees and headed over to my condemned neighbor stealing my attention away from what was about to happen to me.

One of the apes said, "You've been warned, Joey."

"You bastards are savages." He mumbled, with little emotion.

Joey, the Sport Hunter, was like a zombie with rare moments of lucidity. All joy and hope had been drained from him. He was pale with sunken eyes. I wondered how long he had been here. How long did he hold on before despair and quit took him over. I wondered how long it would take before that was me. I couldn't imagine I was too far behind.

"Yeah. Well, coming from you, that doesn't really mean much. Now does it, Joey?"

Another ape used a pair of oversized pliers to pull out each of the steel spikes pinning Joey to his cross. He fell to the ground with a thud.

The ape asked, "Do we have to start counting or are you going to do your job?"

The Sport Hunter picked himself off the ground, looked at me, and took off into the forest. One of the apes blew a horn. The ground shook, signaling that the animals were out in force and ready to hunt their prey.

I turned my attention back to the lion looking directly into his eyes. He had taken a few steps away from me and started to dig at the ground with his paws. I tried to ready and brace myself for the coming attack. But, there was little I could do. I told myself it wasn't real. It wouldn't last long. *You're stronger than they are*, I told myself. *Hold on. You can beat them. You're smarter than they are.*

"You're a monster." He roared.

He leapt, soaring through the air, and landed on me. His plump paws fell atop my shoulders while he simultaneously unsheathed his claws and punctured my skin. The sharp blades came to rest deep in the muscles in my back, striking and bruising my bones. The result was a death grip. Nothing could pry him off me. I slammed my eyes shut. I was helpless, unable to fight back, unable to run, nailed to the cross. He then snapped his jowls tight around my neck. I should have been dead in that instant. Again. Instead, I remained fully aware to experience it all. He tore at my neck and then worked his way to my chest. His slobber soaked me and congealed with my blood. He ate his way to my heart. With each bite and tear, instead of losing consciousness, I lost joy. I lost happiness. I lost hope. I lost any feeling of warmth and love.

Was this what I had contemplated? Was this that monster I so feared, feasting on my soul? If so, my fear was underestimated, but well founded. My dread of nothingness should have paled in comparison to this reality. I had been wrong. This was more than terrifying. This was my soul being torn apart. My soul being annihilated. This wasn't Purgatory. This was Hell.

In between his bites, he screamed directly into my left ear, "You killed me! You stole me from my family! You're the beast, Animal killer. And now you'll pay!" It was so loud my ear drum exploded and bled.

His words confirmed what I suspected. He was the lion I had killed on the African preserve. I kept my eyes tightly closed. I wanted to beg for mercy. I tried to say, "*Please stop. Please.*" But he ripped out my throat from my neck and it now lay on the ground. I couldn't make a sound. Besides, he wasn't wrong. I had done the things he said. Why should he stop? Why would he show me mercy? If I had been him, I would have done all I could do to make me suffer. Nevertheless, when the savage attack continued unmercifully, and without pause, my fear and understanding turned to fury. Instead of pleading for mercy, I wanted to shout, *Fuck you! Fuck you mother fucker! When I get the chance I'm going to rip your fucking heart out and eat it. I'm glad I killed you. I should have killed your whole fucking family.*

But, I couldn't. I wanted to know, how could God allow this to happen to me? This was not love. It seemed like the attack would last forever, but as with the prior attacks, this too ended as abruptly as it began.

"How did that feel?" The lion asked.

I didn't reply. I couldn't. I kept my eyes closed. I refused to give him the satisfaction of acknowledging him. I wondered, how long could this continue? What was the point of all of this? Revenge by a bunch of sick, demented animals. At least when I hunted, I put an end to it. I had not tortured. I was glad I killed them, and I knew, if I could break free, I would figure out how to kill as many of them as I could.

"You can never repay me what you've taken. The worst part is you refuse to understand, and never will. Not really. You call me the beast. You call me the monster. You're the monster."

He shuffled away, unsatisfied.

When I was certain he had left, I violently cried and wailed. Not for him, or in response to his grievances against me, but for my new lot in life. For the agony and assault on my soul. For the torture I was suffering and inevitable destruction of my spirit I assumed would come when they were done with me. I kept my eyes shut. I did not want to feed my terror with the sight of my marred body. And, just like the prior attacks, while I remained, the injuries and wounds to my soul deepened, more of my spirit had been torn away and lost, I was more empty and hollow. This constant barrage since my death was too much to endure. I believed at some point it all had to end. Even if that end came on the other side of the wall behind me. Fulltime despair was devouring me. A little more of me died with each attack. I didn't know how much more of my soul was left to feed them.

After some time, when no further attack came, I decided to open my eyes and survey the damage. I expected to see a mangled mess. I had survived the prior assaults, but this was the most violent yet. I bargained with myself and committed to looking straight ahead. When I gathered the courage, I opened them. But, I couldn't stop myself. I needed to look, to appraise the damage. Incredibly, my body remained uninjured. I was intact. But, the unseen wounds caused by these attacks continued to cut deep. I ached all over. I felt like I had just been in a horrible car accident. Depression and a cloud of profound sadness settled over me.

Looking ahead, I spied a buck looking directly at me from behind a tree. He offered a puzzled look, and then, he smiled. The ground then shook, running him off. I was becoming accustomed to the sound of Azrael's army, but this was different. This sounded like an earthquake, not the march of the army. It was the fourth attack. The thunderous rumble grew louder and closer. The wave of wind hit me first. It was not an animal, but a wall of water that hit me like a tsunami. I shut my eyes and held my breath. I expected to be either dislodged from my cross or that the crucifixion-station itself would be ripped from the ground. Neither happened, and the water did not recede. I was trapped deep underwater. I held my breath for as long as I could. I opened my eyes. My ears popped and hurt. The weight of the water was crushing me. When I could no longer hold my breath, I opened my mouth to search for air. I expected to drown instantly and welcomed the thought. However, I remained alive, nailed to a cross on the bottom of an ocean, drowning endlessly.

When my panic subsided, I caught a swarm in the distance. They huddled together and moved as one mass heading my way. As they neared, I was able to identify that they were hundreds of blue fin tuna. I quickly closed my eyes waiting for it to come. Retribution for the many fishing trips I had taken off the coast of New Jersey and Florida. Bolts of more agony tore at me as they bit and consumed me. Every bite was another gash to my soul. My blood turned the water red. When I thought the attack was over, I opened my eyes. The tuna swam away, but a herd of sharks headed at me. I again closed my eyes and waited. The first shark didn't waste any time. He came from above and bit down on my head, his razor sharp-teeth severing my flesh, veins and nerves, the force so great, it crushed my vertebrae. Terror and sadness are insufficient to describe the impact. The sharks made quick work of me. I was being annihilated bit by bit. The marlins came after the sharks. They used their spear like snouts to pierce and puncture me like a pin cushion. Hundreds of them took turns. With each blow, the will to live and hope drained. Lobsters and shrimp and crab took their turn as well. And, then suddenly they all retreated. The waters then followed and disappeared also. Similar to the prior attacks, my body remained uninjured, but the devastation to my psyche remained. At least on Earth, despair could be conquered by death. Here, there was nothing to make it stop.

The bears came next.

I looked to the foreign sky of this world and again cried to God.

"How can you allow this?"

He didn't answer.

The bears charged fast. It would be the most gruesome attack yet. The relentless onslaught of these attacks were so cruel, designed to crush my spirit. Each attack interrupted any attempt I made to feel sorry for myself. Finally, the attacks ended and the animal army emerged from the surrounding forest. The apes were dragging the Sport Hunter along the ground. He appeared unconscious. His bloody body had several arrows protruding from it. He looked like a life size voodoo doll. They stood him up just right and drove the steel spikes back through him, nailing him back to his cross. He didn't flinch or make a sound.

Azrael watched, looking quite satisfied with himself.

"*Louieee*, you look like you've been enjoying your stay." He said with a wide grin.

"You sick bastard. You condemn me? Look at what you do. Leave me alone."

That spoiled his good mood and got him going.

"Now I've been very patient with you, Louie, but that patience does have its limit. I don't know what makes you think I have to justify my actions to you. I don't know what makes you think I owe you a goddamn thing!" He admonished. "Under the circumstances, I think I've been quite hospitable, all things considered. But manners go only so far. You owe a debt, Louie, and you're *gonna* pay it."

"I've paid it. Enough!" I shouted back.

"Oh come on, Louie. You really are comical. I'll decide when you've paid enough. You see, I'm like the tax man, and the tax man always gets paid. You know what they say, render unto Caesar. You may not like it. You may not agree, but it's your debt nonetheless. And you certainly *ain't talkin* your way out of it. Take a good look what's going on here. This is hard work. It is much more difficult to kill a soul, than an earthly body. It takes time, and effort. You, of all people, should be able to appreciate the skill and dedication I bring to my craft. My army here is properly motivated and patient. And, that's just what we're aiming to do. Kill us some souls. Do you honestly believe you belong in Heaven? You're deluding yourself if you think you ever had a shot at *gettin* in there."

With each word the mammoth elk spoke, hope continued to drain from me. They wounded me almost as much as the seemingly physical attacks. I hated the way he constantly used my name. I did all I could to turn my despair into anger and hatred for this beast tormenting me. As I hung there, I promised myself I would make him pay.

"Just leave me alone." I said.

"Louie, Louie, Louie. Come on now. We're just *gettin* started. Now I know this all seems terribly unfair in your twisted mind, but I assure you this, much more is warranted under the circumstances.

You caused mass suffering, you've got a long way to go to repaying your debt. There are consequences for your conduct. You were a law man, I would think you could appreciate that concept."

"What about forgiveness? Are you that evil?"

"Forgiveness? You want me . . . you want *us* to forgive you? You want God to forgive you? Forgive what? You didn't even do anything wrong. *Ain't* that right, *Louieee*? You know, you first have to ask for forgiveness before you can be forgiven. And more importantly, you have to actually be sorry. That's the fine print everyone always seems to overlook. Forgiveness doesn't come without repentance."

"Okay. I'm sorry." I said curtly.

"You really are a little piss-ant. You've learned nothing. You ask about forgiveness, but you know nothing about it. God forgives, I don't. What *ya* think will happen first, sport? Think me and the boys will forgive you or get bored? Forget about demanding justice and revenge before you see yourself for what you truly are?"

He then lowered his voice to a whisper.

"To be honest, I don't think either of us are *gonna* change our mind anytime soon. And that's the way I like it. My money is on both of us holding out a good real long time. I know you, Louie. I've *seeeen*

all the things you have done. I know who you are.
You *ain't* ever *gettin* where you want to go."

He began to pace around me, I tried not to look
at him.

"I have seen that place. There is no room for the
likes of you and me there. No room at the inn. *Ya*
see, I've been to the Promised Land. I've been to
the mountain top." He said mockingly. "And, I
saw animals and humans playing together, living in
harmony and laughing and loving and respecting
one another."

He really loved to talk. I knew lawyers like that.
They never could figure out when they had made
their point. When the Judge had heard enough,
when it was time to sit down. Azrael did have a
certain cadence and rhythm that could engage any
crowd. It would be almost entertaining, if what he
was saying wasn't so cruel and heartless. I just
hoped the longer I could get him to talk, the longer
my reprieve from the anguish from further assaults.

"But I *ain't* no Moses, and neither are you! That
place *ain't* for you. You wouldn't like it there
anyway. It's filled with peaceful loving creatures.
There *ain't* no *huntin* in Heaven. And I reckon the
Animal Killer wouldn't be happy unless he was
huntin and *killin* him some animals. Go ahead and
tell me I am wrong. Or, have you had a change of
heart? You see the light? You have a come to Jesus

moment? You love me and my kind? You accept us as equals?"

He waited and let the questions linger in the air for a moment.

"Moses never made it into the Promised Land either." I ribbed.

"What was that?"

"I said, Moses never made it into the Promised Land. You said we're not like Moses. Moses never made it to the Promised Land either. What you said made no sense."

"You challenging me, Louie? You trying to agitate me? You think that's wise, given your . . . predicament? Come on, Louie, we both love *huntin*. In another life, who knows, maybe we would've been *huntin* buddies. I think it's time for *sum huntin* now. What'd you say? You up for *sum huntin*?"

"No. Please. Don't. Have mercy–"

"Mercy. You must be *kiddin* me. There you go again using big fancy words you don't understand. No Mercy for you, Louie. Pry his ass down," he told the apes.

It started raining as the wind whipped around.

"*Yeee hawww, nothin* better than *huntin* in some weather. It puts my tracking skills to the test. It's all about the art of the hunt. *Ain't* that right, Louie? It takes some real skill to track your prey in weather."

Two apes approached with pliers and pulled out the metal spikes pinning me to my cross. The process both hurt, while at the same time, released a great deal of my anguish. The rain poured down soaking the ground. I hit the wet dirt, saturated from the rainfall, blood and urine that all mixed together from me, the Sadistic Abuser, and the Sport Hunter. I watched in amazement as my body regenerated and healed, my wounds and bruises disappearing. I sat in the soaked, tainted, mud, looking at my hands astonished.

"Go on. Giddy up, boy." Azrael barked.

"I'm not going anywhere." I replied, remaining on the ground looking up at him.

The Sport Hunter regained consciousness and offered, "Just do what they say. They only make it worse if you don't listen."

Azrael shot him a look.

"Big man shooting his mouth off again? You want us to pry you back down? You can go *runnin* with him," Azrael threatened. "Come on, Louie. Get *goin*. You're free. Run away."

The Twelfth Chapter

I figured I had few choices. I could run or rebel. The Sport Hunter had been here longer and his advice was to run. So I ran. I ran back into and through the sea of trees. I kept slipping and sliding on the wet terrain, falling, smacking against the mud every few feet. The muck and sludge sprayed everywhere, including into my mouth and all over my face. The earthy taste spurring the churning of my stomach, causing it to growl and rumble, reminding it of the sensation of being fed. Famished and thirsty, I continued to run. My fear and frustration worsened when I unwittingly stepped deep into a pool of thick, quicksand-like, mud. I struggled to free myself, and when I did, the suction ripped the shoes I had made from the birch trees, right off both my feet. I turned up to the sky and cursed God. I dismissed any notion of making another pair. There was no time and no point. The physical damage to my feet would mend.

The damage inflicted upon my spirit, on the other hand, I knew would linger. The attacks and crucifixions were methodically eradicating the person I once was. The good news was that with each passing moment of freedom, my march toward the abyss slowed. I continued to put more distance between me and the army. With each step I rebounded. Hope sluggishly returned, but I remained wounded. Every few feet I couldn't help but look back with dread. I knew they were coming. I wondered whether the many deer I had stalked and hunted over the years felt this way. Did they know they were in mortal danger? Centuries of being prey must have informed their DNA, creating an innate knowing, yet unable to do a thing about it.

It was not a pleasant feeling.

Then, the horns blared. Had there been any doubt they were coming for me, the creepy low pitched vibrating buzz ended that. The hunt was on. But even then, the ground didn't tremble. The sky did not darken. There was no thunderous roar of the angry animal army on the march. Everything remained quiet. Only the sound of the rain hitting the trees and mud interrupted the silence. I knew getting far away as possible, as fast as possible, was my only chance. It didn't matter that I had no idea where I was headed. I was going to run until I could run no more. If nothing else, I was free.

I thought about how they would track me and considered the things I would look for if I was on the hunt. The mud would capture my tracks, and like a trail of bread crumbs, guide them right to me. The matted grass, broken branches and snapped twigs on the ground were other tell-tale signs they would use to find me. I would avoid any trails or paths, natural or otherwise. They would expect me to follow them. I wouldn't make that mistake. I wasn't casting a shadow since there was no sun. Hunters will often spot the shadow before the prey themselves. One less thing I would have to worry about. I would also do my best to stay downwind. My human odor, very distinct from theirs, will easily betray me. Also, if I could smell them before they reach me, I can gain the advantage and elude capture. They had the advantage of speed and strength. Not to mention their sheer numbers. But, the air surveillance of the birds above made them a formidable foe. If spotted, they would tattle my position and swarm upon me in moments. My odds of evading capture were not good, but I was determined to never go back. I was regaining my will and fortitude. I reasoned they didn't pursue me immediately; the silence confirmed it. They were giving me a head start. There wouldn't be any sport in hunting me only moments after they let me go. If torment alone was their goal, they could have just continued the butchery while I remained on the cross. No sport in that. This was my opportunity to escape.

Avoiding the animals and disappearing into this unfamiliar alien world required that I first put as much distance between me and them; so, for the time being, I didn't worry about covering my tracks. I simply ran to create distance. I longed for fresh camouflage. It would help conceal and warm me. The constant cold ruthlessly seared my soul. Everything in this world, one way or another, was a perpetual assault on my spirit. I recalled the time I had brought a cardboard box with me on a hunting trip. I sat on the ground under the box, able to hide in plain sight. My prey, the deer, would saunter right up to me, unknowing that their executioner lie hiding beneath. They were easy pickings. I could use something like that now. The apes had bows and arrows, no rifles, so they would have to get relatively close to me. *Maintain your distance*, I kept telling myself as I ran.

After an unknowable passage of time, I stopped running. My lungs burned, back ached and legs shook, despite the adrenaline pumping through me. I paused to listen for them. Still nothing. There was no buzz from the horns. No thunderous march. Just the pitter patter of the rain failing. I looked around panting, trying to catch my breath, contemplating my next move. I surveyed the muddied tracks I had left behind. *They're going to be on you fast if you continue like this.* My heart banged violently at the thought.

Shaking my head, I whispered, "I can't go back. I have to do something different."

The constant barrage of the attacks was a hell I could no longer endure. *Those bastards freed me intentionally for a purpose. They want to stalk me for the sport of it.* I was disgusted at the thought. This was meant to maximize the terror, barbarity and brutality of the hunt. Maximize their revenge. Their method, heartless and cruel, dangled hope just beyond my reach. I suspected they would snatch it away long before it was in my grasp. I fought the inclination to succumb to the terror and did all I could to replace it with anger. I needed to retain my wits.

For all I knew, several members of Azrael's army were already strategically positioned around these killing fields, waiting for me to walk into their ambush. That's what I would have done. I would simply set up a tree stand downwind and just wait, let them come to me. That's when the idea struck. This part of the dense wilderness was not populated with fully grown, mature trees, but they were perfect to carry out my idea; tall enough and close to one another. *That'll work*, I smiled, locating a tree whose branches I could reach with a small jump. The rain made it difficult, but I grabbed on and managed to pull myself up. I climbed higher to where the branches were thicker and stronger. Everything was wet, making it difficult to maneuver. As I climbed, I slipped and shrieked, "Son of a bit–" but caught myself, muffling the sound, and regaining my grip before I fell. Eventually, I succeeded scaling the wet bark. I was a man on a mission. The trees grew so close, their limbs were like interlocking fingers holding hands. This made it easy to move from tree to tree. The fingers served as my bridge in the sky. I made my way from tree to tree. Many of the branches were not very thick and I was concerned stepping onto the wrong one would result in a serious fall. I was also concerned that the noise of the cracking and rustling branches and leaves would reveal my whereabouts. But, of my few options, this was best. My tracks would suddenly disappear confusing them. It would buy me time and distance. I made my way through the woodland for several hundred yards before making my way back down to the now saturated mushy ground.

I desperately wanted to rest, but I knew that would be a mistake. I battled feelings of hopelessness, a challenge, because despite my returning strength and will, I didn't realistically see a way out. After all, when all was said and done, I was battling God. Not a fight I could win. I wavered, wanting to just give up. Call it quits. I didn't want this anymore. I would end my own life if I could, but, I couldn't even control that. I continued on, mired in my pity when I was struck with the most hopeful thought. I was wrong, I could end this. I could offer myself to the Spirit Destroyer. The idea excited me. If I could somehow make it back to the gate and break open those doors, I could end this. If God was done with me, I would give Him what He wanted. I stopped and turned back toward the direction I had come. I would not allow them the satisfaction of hunting me down. While I convinced myself that this was a good plan, heading straight back was not. I would run directly into Azrael and never get the chance to break open those doors. I would have to work my way around and out flank the army. If I could do that, I would head straight to those doors. Nothing would stop me. For the first time since my exile, I smiled. I set aside feeling sorry for myself, I was determined to fight. If I couldn't escape, at least I had a plan. The hope I might be able to end my torment reinvigorated me. This could actually end.

I ran a little further before attempting to circle back. I came to a sweeping cluster of vividly green covered hills. As I ascended the one closet to me, the sky turned a magnificent deep dark blue. It reminded me of the still water of the South Mid Atlantic. When disturbed, it would reveal the tropical turquoise below. Unchurned, it held a unique blue, seen nowhere else on Earth. This sky mirrored that blue. It seemed to have changed with my mood. I felt calmed. The sudden scented breeze from the wildflowers of purple Lavender, Aster and Senna flowers floated through the air. Maybe, the aroma had been there all along and I just hadn't noticed it before. When I reached the top of the hill I saw an extensive depression in the terrain below covering several hundred acres surrounded by hills on all sides. Barn-like structures of varying sizes and shapes littered the terrain. The animal army barracks, I thought. Apparently, I haplessly made my way right to the lion's den so to speak. Hell's home base.

To me, Azrael was the devil. If the Destroyer would put an end to this, I considered that mercy. But Azrael, he was the ring master of this circus, he enjoyed inflicting the pain. I squatted down to avoid being discovered and crawled on my belly to make my way closer. The compound housed countless animals. Closer, I watched animals of every shape and size fight with one another. The grounds were soaked with blood. The stench of rotting carcasses and spoiled blood overpowered the sweet scent of the wildflowers. I watched a bear destroy a Zebra. The Zebra was still alive when the bear started to feast on him. The cold overtook me again and I shuddered. Hunger and thirst followed, weakening me with desire. I had come to understand that I no longer needed these things in my current form to survive, but I still craved food and water. Their lack intensified my anguish.

I quickly formed a plan that made use of my hunting skills. I carefully crawled away from the animal enclave and found the perfect size branch to use as a spear. I snapped the branch at its end and rubbed the broken end against a large flat rock. With some effort, I formed a fairly sharp point at the tip. When I was satisfied I could make it no sharper, I stored the weapon against a tree. Then I took the flat rock and struck and ground it against a larger rock until it formed a sharp edge. I placed it next to the spear. Under the trees were countless dead fallen leaves covering the terrain. I smiled. Still covered in wet mud, I rolled through the leaves. They clung to the mud. I had my camouflage, a natural canopy. It was the next best thing to real camo. I hoped, as I crawled on my belly back toward a group of fawns huddled around the back of the compound, that I would blend into the landscape and avoid detection. One fawn lingered near the pen fence. The others were several yards away and had their back turned to it. I crawled an inch at a time. When I was at the fence I held my breath. I gently extended my arm, and when my hand was near its hind leg, I grabbed it and yanked as hard as I could. He fell on his side and I pulled him away. For a moment he was stunned, but that was short lived. Once the initial shock wore off, he began to struggle and violently thrash about. I grabbed him by the snout and kept his mouth closed. I headed back to the cover of the trees awkwardly on my knees. Then I got up and I ran while holding the fighting fawn.

"Stop resisting or I'll snap your neck right here. I've done it before," I whispered, not knowing if he would understand.

The fawn immediately stopped struggling, but I continued to hold his snout so he couldn't scream. I managed to disappear behind the trees on the hill without being discovered by any of the animals roaming around the garrison.

When we finally made it back to where I had left the spear, I asked, "You understand me?"

He shook his head up and down to indicate that he did.

"Good. You see that spear? You see that shaved sharp rock on the ground? You see them both, don't you?"

He again motioned his head to indicate that he did.

"I am going to let go of your mouth. If you make any sound– cry for help, or try to run I'm going to grab that spear and put it in you. And then, I'm going to cut your throat with that rock. Got it?"

He again motioned that he did.

Still holding on to him, I let go of his snout, I reached down and grabbed the spear.

"Good, now I am going to put you down. I just want some answers and then I'll let you go. Deal?"

He again indicated that he understood. I had no intention to harm him. In that instant I knew my hunting and hurting days were most likely done. All I wanted now was to end this, end the suffering. Taking a leap of faith, I put him down. I still held the spear and pointed it menacingly at him, just in case.

"You got a name?" I asked.

"I do. Call me Enzo."

"Enzo, I'm Lou." I searched for any sign of recognition from him. There was none.

"How do I get out of here, Enzo?"

"Out of here? You don't. There is no out of here, not unless you have the lamb, they'll negotiate for the lamb."

"I don't have any lamb. Please– there must be someplace I can go. At least tell me how I can reach Karma. I think he made a mistake. I'm not supposed to be here."

"These guys don't make mistakes." He said shaking his head. "And there's no place to go. At least not any place I know. I'd be there already if there was. This place is hell."

"Come on, give me something. Why are you here? What do you want from me? How do I end this?"

"*Uhh*, slow down there, Lou. I don't want anything from you. You just grabbed me, remember? I don't know you, right? I'm just trying to survive myself. What I do know is that one minute I was like you, and then the next, I was tried and convicted by the Deciders and I woke up in this place as an animal."

"What do you mean you were like me?"

"I was human. I was a man."

I offered a blank stare.

"It's true. I was human. Now I'm not. Now I'm a prisoner," he said, his voice quivering as his eyes darted about.

I didn't know what to make of this.

He continued, "That's not the worst of it. This Azrael and his goons surround me moments after I arrive here and he informs me that I have two choices: I can join his army fighting for God, rendering judgment on the condemned, *blah blah blah*, or, I can be slaughtered and used to feed his army."

"That's rough, Enzo, but take my word, you got off easy."

"Doesn't feel so easy. Doesn't feel easy at all, constantly hunting guys like you– and the lambs."

"I know what you mean, trust me." I offered.

I was thinking fast, as I looked back down at the blood bath below, I needed to learn something and move on.

"How did that bear kill that zebra?" I motioned with my chin in the direction of the garrison. "I didn't think anything died in this place. I've been tortured for so long, I should have been dead a long time ago, and yet, here I am."

"I hate to be the one to break it to you– you're already dead."

"I know, it's an expression. The zebra?" I insisted.

"There's different rules for of each of us. This place isn't all about you. It's a giant chess board. Each of us is a pawn, all serving a different purpose, while serving our sentence.

"And, what's with this lamb you keep talking about?"

"Azrael, he is obsessed. He makes us hunt for the lambs day and night. There's one left. He slaughters them. That zebra down there refused to do it any longer. You want out, give up the lamb. Azrael rewards those who bring him one." He began to shiver again.

"Why, what does Azrael have against lambs?"

"I don't know– the . . . the last person to ask that question, ended up like the zebra."

"Last question. How do I open the gate to the Spirit Destroyer?"

He shook his head. "Sorry. Can't help with that one either. I just heard when they deliver someone to him, you don't want to be anywhere near there when those doors open. Nothing escapes."

The sound of the birds moving toward us broke in, distracting us. We both looked up. The thunderous roar got closer.

"I got to get out of here. If I let you go, can I trust you not to tell them I was here?"

"No worries, Lou. You won't get any trouble from me. I just want to get out of here alive myself."

"Thanks. Good luck, Enzo."

"Good luck, Louie."

I turned and ran toward a thicker band of trees still holding onto their leaves. I hugged the largest one I could find, hoping to blend in and hide. I had spent far too long questioning Enzo. I had no doubt Azrael and his army were now scouring the landscape. It was only a matter of time before I would be caught. Then I froze, I turned back for a moment. My hand reflexively shot up to my mouth and my heart erratically beat against my chest. Enzo called me Louie. I told him my name was Lou. I had no idea if I would be betrayed. All the more reason to move fast. When the birds were gone, I sprinted in what I thought was the direction away from the pursuing army and animal compound. I headed toward the unknown, uncharted, expanse ahead. I wasn't sure where I was going or if there was a safe place to be found, but I was determined to try. My mind wandered and before I knew it, the lush green vegetation and grass began to fade and brown. The trees became sparse. I lost my cover from the birds and was now completely exposed. The grass and dwindling foliage continued to become more brown, brittle and dry. Before I knew it, I was on the precipice of a desert. The rain receded and air dried. I cursed my fortunes. Like the mud before it, the desert sand ahead would record my every step. It was too dangerous to turn back. I pressed on hoping wind and time would wash away my tracks imprinted into the sand below.

I was furious with myself for trusting Enzo. I feared he would turn on me, revealing that I had been in the area and share what I had asked about. I hoped not. Night began to consume the sky. The desert terrain was hilly and difficult to traverse. I stumbled and fell every few feet, sinking into the sandy ground. I couldn't resist but to look behind me every minute or so to see if the animals picked up my trail and were closing in. I was so consumed with what might be lurking behind me that I neglected to heed what was ahead. I lost my footing and tumbled and slid down a steep decline. When the momentum of my fall subsided, I came to a stop inches before I went over the side of a tall cliff. An enormous ridge lay, hundreds of feet below, stranded between two mountainous hills.

The sky darkened and the dusty air soured, acquiring a putrid noxious heated texture. The odor of beef frying in a pan of bacon fat, but spoiled by sulfur and a tinge of burnt liver assaulted my senses. I pinched my nose closed with my fingers, holding my hand over my mouth, trying not to breathe too deeply. I knelt down and peeked over the side of the drop to get a better view. Below, a vast bubbling caldron, a volcano-like pit ready to erupt. The orange and red soup of magma was so hot, flames shot up every few seconds singeing the air. I shook my head thinking, *this is hell*. Even though the heat baked the atmosphere, my perpetual chill retained its death grip. Movement in the distance on the other side of the ridge caught my attention. I made my way around to get a closer look. About halfway there, I saw a giant wooden wall and my heartbeat quickened again. It was the same size and type of wall that contained the Spirit Destroyer. I had thought I journeyed away from his lair, but must have somehow lost my bearings and circled back. There were similar bronze doors on this part of the wall, however, these doors were propped open. A troop of apes diligently worked, dragging dead human bodies out of the destroyer's sanctum. They tossed the carcasses into one of two growing mass graves. Another troop then worked on emptying one of the graves, tossing the discarded bodies into the caldron of hell fire. As each body hit the flame, it vaporized instantly. The apes then dragged the body of the Sadistic Abuser from the lair. The man who had been nailed on the crucifix two down from me. They tossed him into the grave without pause or pity. I never did ask him his name. Was this to be my fate as well? Tortured, extinguished and then incinerated? Is that how it will end? Seeing this made me reconsider my plan to present myself to the Destroyer. Nauseated, my respiration quickened, chilled and wet from my sweat, I turned and ran.

With the mass crematorium and desert behind me and no sign of the army, I decided to rest. I came to a new landscape and propped myself down against a tree and closed my eyes. I realized it was only the second time it had turned dark since I had come to this place. That couldn't be right. I felt like it's been weeks since my death. Certainly days. I came to understand that a day in this place wasn't the same as it is on Earth. *What is that saying in the Bible, that one day with the Lord is as a thousand years, and a thousand years as one day.* Something like that I remembered. Time ticked like that in this place. Even though the ongoing annihilation was well behind me, the warm air carried the sickening smell of burning flesh and bone. I repressed the urge to gag. I just wanted to sleep, needed to sleep. I wanted to be a kid again playing baseball, consuming the summer scents of fresh cut grass and hotdogs and barbeques, or at least dream about it, instead of facing the malodorous stench of death. I wanted to hold my wife. I wanted to lie down with my head in her lap with her stroking my hair. I had always loved that. With these thoughts floating through my mind, finally, I fell asleep.

Sadly, sleep provided no escape from my suffering. A menagerie of nightmares taunted me, chasing away my earlier thoughts of the past. Lions chasing and tackling me, tearing at my flesh.

Squirrels and rats eating my eyes while I was tied down. Cats and dogs feasting on my dead corpse lying in the snow covered woods. It ended with Karma looking at me and shouting, *"Run, Louie, Run!"* I shot up in unfamiliar surroundings, briefly forgetting I was hell. Then I heard the crack of a twig. My heart jammed into my throat. I froze and listened. The dark was gone, it was light again.

I then heard a whisper, compounding my panic. "This way."

I jumped to my feet and tried to determine direction of the voice. But it went quiet. Which was more unnerving than the sound that startled me. I had to move. I took off, sprinting. A moment later, that sound again, the *whoosh*. A flying arrow cut through the air. It just missed the back of my head and embedded itself in the tree ahead of me. I started to zig zag and headed toward a dense group of trees hoping for cover from the huntsman pursuing me. I kept telling myself, *you're going to make it. You're going to make it.* Then, I repeated it out loud. I berated myself for not swallowing my fear and present myself to the Spirit Destroyer, or better yet, cast myself into the crematorium pit when I had the chance. Hope unfairly seduced me. I would not make that mistake again. I would escape and head straight to that pit. The hope I would be able to carry out my plan shattered the moment the first arrow hit my back. More damage to my already wounded soul. I kept running. Then I heard something moving through the air. It sounded large. I looked up and over my shoulder. The sky darkened. At first, I thought it was starting to rain again. I wasn't that lucky. It was a lethal storm of arrows pouring down hell and fury. I was struck between my shoulder and neck. That injury instantly debilitated me. I fell to the ground and crawled. I had to keep moving. I couldn't go back. Another arrow pierced my hand, impaling it to the ground. There were too many of them. The animals were on me in an instant. A lion grabbed my arm in his mouth, his fangs puncturing my flesh. The force cracked my ulna bone. He dragged me, tearing my hand from the arrow pinning it. I was helpless to make him stop.

"No. No." I cried.

Azrael emerged from the masses that surrounded me.

"I must say, I am quite impressed. You gave us a good run. That took a bit longer than I expected. Good for you. I always appreciate good effort. I never grow tired of the rush I get while *trackin* my prey. You know, once you've marked it. Once you've made up your mind he's the one. Then, the rush of the chase. But, let's be honest, there *ain't* nothing better than the absolute thrill of the kill itself. That moment of complete conquest. Don't you agree, *Louieeee*?" He mockingly said, waiting for a response. I offered him none.

"Come on, Louie, you know exactly what I am talking about. The rush. Nothing beats the rush."

The Lion continued to drag me by his mouth while Azrael followed along taunting me.

"But I do hope you improve at this, Louie. In fact, I'm *gonna* have to insist you do. We've got a lot of time together and I would just hate *gittin* bored *huntin* you."

The arrows still implanted in my back dug deeper as the lion dragged me along. My fortitude quickly dissolved, making it impossible tamp down the raw emotion. I erupted in a wail and cried, giving him the satisfaction I hoped to deny him. My mouth, locked in an open gasp, a visceral howl of mourning gushed from deep within me. When we arrived back, I continued to sob uncontrollably, but that didn't stop the apes from lifting me up and nailing me back to my crucifix.

Azrael smiled, watching with pleasure.

"*Awww*, come on, Louie. Don't you know there *ain't* no *cryin* in *huntin*? What is it with your family? Bunch of crybabies. *Ya* know, I welcomed your daddy here also. He hung with us a real long time. We had a good time with that one. He was a cry baby too."

Anger filled me. The mention of my father set me into an outright rage. I struggled to tear through the spikes holding me back.

"That's not true, you motherfucker. You say you do the work of God? This is not God's work. You're the sadistic abuser. You enjoy torture. You're demented."

I shouted through tears and snot and the pain of the metal spikes that kept reopening unbearable wounds. One of the apes yanked out the arrows still imbedded in me as I screamed.

"Don't you dare tell me what I am. I know exactly what I am. And, by now, you should know exactly what I am capable of. What makes you think I am interested in what a little piss-ant like you thinks? Who are you, Louie? You forfeited your right a long time ago to judge me or anyone else. You're the monster and a hypocrite. I am what I am. But you, Louie, you lie to yourself. You lied to everyone around you. You went to church and prayed to God while you tortured and killed His creation, and bragged about it. I'm *doin* God's work. What are you *doin*, Louie? I know what I am. I don't need you to tell me. The bigger question is who are you, Animal Killer?"

"Listen to me. I'm sorry. I really am. I mean it. I get it now." I pleaded.

Animal Killer

"You make me laugh, Louie. Forgive and forget huh? That's what we should do?"

"Yes. God commands forgiveness."

"You *preachin* the Gospel now, *Louieee*? *Wooo hooo,* I am impressed. Louie, has found religion. Only problem for you, sport, is forgiveness is for those who repent. You repenting?"

"Yes. I am."

"Now, why is it I don't believe you? It doesn't come that easy. *Ya* know, I may talk a little slow sometimes, but that don't mean I think slow. You're going to have to do a lot better than that," he said, watching me as I struggled on the crucifix.

I was crushed. I was beginning to understand. Maybe not completely to my core. But, I now understood these were living breathing creatures with feelings. Hearing them speak and reveal their feelings, and having lived through the reenactments of their slaughters, brought unwelcomed understanding. I was becoming sorry. I never saw it that way, the way things actually are.

"You curse me, Louie, but you remain blind. I hunt to do God's will, you hunt for fun, for a trophy. You hunt to put a stuffed head on your wall. Oh, Louie, how I weep for you. You have no clue, you're your own worst enemy. You've been *killin* and depriving your own soul since your birth.

Long before I got my spikes into you. You have been storing up God's wrath. With every kill, you moved closer to the abyss. You owe a debt- now it's time for God to collect."

I writhed on the cross, pulling and tearing at the spikes as I bit my tongue.

"Let me ask, those you slaughtered, where do you think they are now? Dust? Gone? No, Louie, I tell you, on this very day, those that are not here, are in the Kingdom. They enjoy eternal bliss. But look at you, it is you who now suffers. Not at the whim of what you call a sadistic monster, but by your own actions. Your choices. You've done all this to yourself. You have much blood on your hands and your ignorance is only surpassed by your arrogance. That'll all change though once I'm done with *ya* and the Destroyer does his work. In fact, since you're so keen on telling me who I am, let me confirm it for you."

He turned to the apes, "Get him back down."

"No. I'm sorry! You're right. I'll stop."

The apes removed the spikes with amazing ease, throwing me off the cross. I collapsed to the ground, exhausted.

"It's too late for sorry. I'm *gonna* show you exactly who I am." Azrael snarled, so angry he wouldn't look at me.

Animal Killer

Everything went dark. I woke up in a jungle a moment later. I slowly stood and surveyed the setting. Confused how I got here, I had no idea where I was in relation to where I had been. A new wave of hunger and thirst made me unsteady. I then remembered Azrael's words, *I'm gonna show you exactly who I am.* He was enraged. *How far behind were they? How bad was this going to be?* I knew they were out there. They were coming for me. I felt like the deer of the mountains and woods surveying the descending army of hunters at the start of every killing season; they knew they were coming for them, but there was nothing they could do stop it. The knowing increased the terror.

Frightening cackles coming from unseen hyena erupted all around me. I couldn't determine the direction of the laugh-like cries. My hands shook violently. I was fixated on how they trembled. I had always had a steady hand. Now, I couldn't calm them. The manifestation of the unrelenting fear, the unrelenting assaults. I was frazzled, my nerves raw and exposed. I expected this to be the worst assault yet. I ran. I heard them running all around me. Wolves howled, announcing they joined the chase. The roars from the tigers followed. I heard them all, but saw none. I could never outrun them. Hunting was most certainly in their DNA, and I was easy prey. They taunted me, remaining concealed. Tears streamed down my face.

The fear became too much to contain, my knees weakened and legs folded. I fell to the ground. I pushed my face against the moist dirt and overgrown grass, screaming as loud as I could. I knew they were there, but there was nothing I could do. I was surrounded by an unending number of oversized wolves, tigers and hyena. There were hundreds, maybe thousands of them. They all held misplaced merciless grins and salivated excessively. The hyena laughed with terrifying high pitched screeches. Then, they pounced, shredding and tearing me apart. It was quick, but mean, violent work. The ferocity of this attack was so great, for the first time I saw parts of my soul torn away. Several bursts of dazzling white light escaped from my remains and sped up into the sky. I felt emptier than I had ever before, lighter, like there was less of me. I wanted to cry, but couldn't. Maybe that was the part they destroyed. I wasn't sure. When finished, they dragged me back to my cross.

The Thirteenth Chapter

The apes ruthlessly hammered the steel spikes through my wrists and ankles skewering and anchoring me to my crucifix. With the clang of each strike, the spikes drove deeper into me and I died a little more. I hung impaled, bleeding from my wounds. Azrael looked on with satisfaction, convinced he was fulfilling God's will. The worst part, the thing that made this all most difficult to endure, was the absence of any sign of hope for a future free from this suffering. There was no light at the end of the tunnel. My existence consisted of grotesque misery for an interminable term. And when they were done, they would present me to the Destroyer who would eviscerate me and toss my remains into a lake of fire, obliterated and hidden far away from anyone who had ever cared for me.

I screamed out against the pain and against that which awaited me. I screamed long and loud for all the mistakes I had made. I had been blind. I caused immeasurable suffering. There was no denying that. At the least, God was decidedly not pleased with me. Once Azrael departed I dove deeper into despair. Karma and the Deciders lied to me. Or at least they had not been completely honest. They told me they would see me again. It appeared they would not. I wept for this world. I wept for the wrong I had committed against God. It was not my intention. It was my ignorance, and arrogance, as Azrael charged. And now, God had abandoned me, leaving me to rot in this hell. I mostly wept for my own agony. But then, in the distant recess of my mind, the foggy frail fragment of something short of hope tugged, continuing the sea saw ride of emotion. My plan. I returned to my plan. If I could free myself, I would end my suffering. It wasn't redemption. It wasn't an escape. It was an end. An end I welcomed and a chance I was determined not miss again.

With all that had happened, with all I had seen and with all that had been revealed to me, it shouldn't come as a surprise I questioned the morality of my lifelong convictions. The consequences of despair are tried and true. My sustained dejection sledgehammered at the foundations of my beliefs, shattering and dismantling the illusions I had created. I was beginning to form new understandings and priorities. Those that I should have, and could have, seen before, but didn't, wouldn't. The insight I gained was so basic and elemental, I'm embarrassed I lacked it before. I've come to realize that things, particularly conquests and pride, mean nothing. All that matters is what we do with the parts of the world we borrow.

I want to believe that had I known my fate, I would have done things differently. But, I'm not sure that's true. I suspect, had I been told I was being cruel and offending God, I would have simply dismissed and ignored the admonitions and warnings. Had I been told I would suffer this damnation, sadly, I would have laughed. Without concrete evidence, without the actual experience, I would not have changed a thing. I would not have believed. So many of life's most important lessons cannot be taught. Not by a teacher. Not by a parent. And certainly not by a priest. Certain lessons come only from time and experience, no matter the warnings. Our ego is a clever liar. It spins fairy tales, clouding our thinking. It emboldens us to charge forward, even in the face of God's wrath. We do this because our pride blossoms and blinds us to His will. And then, reality hits; it is only then that despair goes to work.

I thought about just how hard it is to be human. The things we do to ourselves. The things we do to each other. Unspeakable things. Unholy, ungodly things. I think that is why so many have turned away from God. It is much easier to justify our actions. To not have to account. To not have to live up to a standard. To be free to live life by our own code of conduct. Our own standard. We delude ourselves and say if there were a God, He would not allow this or that to happen, when all the while it is us creating the world in which we live. We think that as long as we live by our standard of what is good, of what is right and wrong, then that should be good enough. Blissfully and intentionally ignorant that our actions lead to our damnation. Blind and deliberately myopic to the fact that this thinking leads to being nailed to a cross and slowly slaughtered for eternity, unable to escape it. There is no suicide from this place. No place to run. No drug to take. Nothing to do but look into the face of retribution while the abyss waits for me a few yards behind a wall. Unforgiving. Unrelenting. I ignored the warnings. I obviously ignored the teachings of God. I still didn't want to accept the imposed penalty for my sins. I still resisted, finding it difficult to swallow eternal damnation as the price for killing an animal.

"Why have you forsaken me?" I shouted to the sky through tears.

Animal Killer

The cry sounded fake and cliché, given the circumstances and my predicament.

"Why don't you just shut up already! Stop your crying," the Sport Hunter ordered. "Come on– what did you think was going to happen? You think crying about it now is going to do anything for you? Accept it. Haven't you figured out yet why you are here? Now keep quiet, and allow me to suffer in peace."

I didn't respond. Instead, I fell back into my catatonic trance. It was more vivid than a day dream. My eyes were open, but I was someplace else. I was running through the snow and being followed, but I didn't know by what. I kept looking behind me, but didn't see anything. I was out of breath and trying to get home to my family. A constant dread hung over me. I made it to my house and peaked through a cracked window in the back. My family just sat down to have dinner. There was a place setting at the head of the table where I had always sat. Every meal at our home was an event. Every night was like a holiday feast. Most families today rarely have dinner together. When they do, they spend their time looking down at their smartphones while nibbling on some takeout or microwaved frozen processed dinner. Not at our house.

The long rectangular table gave the family and any neighbor or friend that stopped by plenty of room to join us. I saw the big bowl containing our usual fresh arugula salad with a dash of salt, pepper and fresh squeezed lemon. We always ate the salad with the meal or after, never before. We never understood the American tradition of eating it first. Who wanted to fill up on salad? Next, was the big plate of meatballs with a nice crust and char from the skillet. Our homemade sauce lay next to it. We made the best sauce. Every year, the family would get together for an entire weekend and we would jar a year's worth of our own sauce using tomatoes from our backyard and bales of fresh tomatoes we purchased from a farm in New Jersey near my cousin's house. We pressed the tomatoes using a fifty year old machine that was permanently infused with a fresh tomato scent and stained red. We placed the sauce into mason jars with a basil leaf and kept it in cold storage in the basement. The scent of garlic frying in olive oil escaped the kitchen and reached me, causing my stomach to pang with desire.

Before I could see what else was on the table the vision exploded. Azrael rammed his antlers into my chest. I was so enthralled in the day dream, I didn't see him coming. The violent collision should have killed me instantly, or at least wounded me mortally. Instead, I gasped as the blow compressed my chest, forcing me to let go of all my breath. The resulting damage was yet another trauma to my soul. The aftermath was deeper despair and fading hope for something better, or at least an end to this insufferable torment and misery. The vision reminded me of all I had lost and how far I had fallen. I trembled with an overwhelming sense of loss as the vision faded completely.

"Where'd you go, Louie? You sleeping? Dreaming? Haven't you figured out yet that you don't need sleep here? Dream all you want, sport, there *ain't* no escape. We decided we're *gonna* mix it up. We're *gonna* have ourselves what I like to call a twofer. The two of you are *gonna* run together this time."

The apes stepped forward and pried me and the Sport Hunter off our crosses. We both fell to the ground with a thud. While our bodies may have been unharmed, the will to run wasn't there. The only thing that kept me going was my plan to end this.

"Go on. Get *goin*." Azrael ordered.

I understood there was no point in arguing or pleading. There was no bargaining. No one wanted to listen to me complain. We both stood and ran without protest. I let the Sport Hunter take the lead. I decided for the time being I would keep my plan a secret. I was determined not to do anything to jeopardize its success. This needed to end.

We ran until we reached just beyond the tree line. Once we were hidden, the Sport Hunter broke stride and began to walk. He was deliberate with each step and knew exactly where he was headed. I wondered if he knew something about this place that could help us escape. A way out that he just hadn't been able to reach.

"Where we going?" I asked.

He ignored me and continued to navigate the foothills and debris of fallen branches and puddles. He walked like a man who didn't have a care in the world, like a man taking a walk in the park. Not like a man being hunted.

"Hey. I asked a question."

"Just follow me." He rebuked.

He was a shell of a man. I wasn't too far away from being that dead myself. But, I was committed to never allow things to get that far for me.

"Shouldn't we be trying to cover our tracks?" I suggested.

"Wouldn't matter."

We came to a fork in the road. He turned right, heading east. I was convinced east was the direction from where I had first entered this place, toward the waterfall I had survived. I wanted to go left and head west, to explore if there was some way to escape, or some sanctuary from the animals.

"Hey. What about this way?" I pointed to the left.

"No. Never go that way. I was told if I ever went that way, the consequences would be severe."

"Severe? Are you kidding me? What could possibly be worse than what they've been doing?"

"*Ehh.*" He grunted. "Good point. I don't know how things could get worse. I don't want to know and I'm not about to find out. They keep their promises."

His voice was soft and monotone, as if he had already given up.

"How long you been here?" I asked.

"No idea. I quit asking them. When I did, they laughed at me, and said time had no meaning in this place. What I know is many others have come and gone while I remain. The good news is, Azrael told me this was my last time. He has said it before, to mess with me, but I believe him this time."

"What does that mean?"

"It means I am getting fed to that Spirit Destroyer. It's over for me." He turned to me with his sullen, sunken, sad eyes. "When it happens, pray for me. There's no one to pray for me. I think I've been dead for so long, my few family members have passed on themselves. Maybe I'm wrong about that, but I'm sure they've stopped praying for me by now. It doesn't seem right. No one knows what's about to happen to me. That I go alone."

He turned and continued weaving up and over the hills and through the forest. I followed.

"What did the Deciders tell you?" I asked.

"Who remembers? Who cares? I remember they said that it was just that I suffer. Imagine that. It's just that I suffer. They told me it was unlikely that I would make it, but they hoped they would see me again."

I thought about that. *Had I heard them wrong? Is that what they said to me? They hoped they would see me again, or did they say they would?* Now, I couldn't recall.

"How bad do you think it is on the other side of that wall?" I asked.

He paused and turned around.

"I've heard it." He lowered his voice to a whisper. "I was never around when someone was brought in, but I heard it afterwards. Terrifying screams. The place lights up like it's the Fourth of July. And when the screams reach their climax, there's a flash, like an atom bomb exploding. Then suddenly, it gets real quiet when it's done. It sounds real bad. But I welcome it. I've done what I've done. Time to get on with it."

"I am ready for it too. But, I'd rather escape if I can."

I continued to fall into the trap. Each time I had been freed, hope fooled me, causing me to move toward escape, rather than doing all I could to end it with the Destroyer. I had to resist hope's call.

"Escape? There's no escape. I've tried everything. I've searched almost every inch of this hell. There is no way out," he told me as he stumbled onward.

The somber mood turned more somber while I continued to follow his lead for the time being. Then, I heard a growing swell.

"What's that noise?" I asked.

"Just follow me."

He didn't seem concerned. As we continued, the sound became louder and clearer. It was the crash of ocean waves. We emerged from the dense forest onto a magnificent beach. Ocean as far as the eye could see.

"Why did you bring me here? We're trapped. I thought you were going to help? I thought we were trying to get away." I said agitated and filled with fraught.

"I wanted to see the ocean one last time before I'm no more. There is no getting away. This is Hell, and there is no escape. No second chances. Besides, I can't do anything to jeopardize going to the

Destroyer. I just wanted to see the water one last time," he said sounding sad and tired, but somehow accepting of it all.

He sat down and stared at the distant horizon. Watching the waves crest and crash. The salt air hitting his face. He smiled for the first time since I met him. He seemed at peace. I wondered if there was freedom out there over the horizon.

Suddenly, they emerged from the forest in a swarm. I first noticed them down the beach to my right. I turned to my left and watched as they marched from that direction too. The animals found us. There were so many of them. A sea of animals. I turned back to the forest and took a step, but that's when I heard the rustling and that sudden *whoosh* again. A thousand flying arrows launched from a firing squad obscured behind the trees met me, penetrating my body. Another explosion of agony and helplessness claimed me. I fell to the ground, writhing in pain.

Azrael emerged and stood over me like a conquering hero. A dozen or so apes surrounded the Sport Hunter. He didn't say a word and kept his gaze on the ocean for as long as he could before the apes snatched him up. I managed to get to my knees. Azrael was accompanied by his usual collection of merry mammals and sycophants, with the endless sea of the army assembling in every direction behind him, spread out for miles. I noticed the same animals always stood closest to Azrael. His inner circle so to speak, but this time there was one deer standing awkwardly close to him. One I had not seen before.

An arrow was lodged in my left eye and my throat. I surveyed the new deer through my one good eye, through the pain and anguish. The deer's eyes narrowed and his jowls clenched. His breathing became more rapid and his massive torso expanded and contracted to accommodate his quickened respiration. Azrael, who had been eyeing the Sport Hunter, turned his attention back to me, but I would swear, just before he did, this other deer winked at me. I thought maybe I imagined it.

"You really are a little piss-ant." Azrael said in disgust. "That's your one and only strike, Animal Killer. Next time–"

I looked away.

"Hey!" He shouted.

My head involuntarily jerked and twisted back toward him at the sound of the shout.

"You look at me when I'm *talkin* to you, boy! I was *sayin* . . . next time . . . you'll do better or there will be . . . consequences."

He turned to an ape and tilted his head, pointing his antlers to the Sport Hunter.

"Take that one back. His time is up. Deliver him to our friend."

"I hate you." I cried.

"*Louieee*, you ought to trust me, I'm excellent at delivering justice– that one there is *gettin* everything he deserves."

"Screw you. Screw all of you!" I shouted. The creatures stared back stoically. "You want me to feel bad about what I did? Look at how you treat me now. I am glad I did what I did. You're a masochist. You all are! How long must I suffer? Where's your mercy? Where's your forgiveness? When is enough, enough?"

"Oh, Louie, we have so much more time together for me to show you my mercy. I will miss you though when you're gone. But for now, we're just *gettin* started. We're just *gettin* warmed up. The real fun is coming, just you wait and see."

He turned to the deer standing beside him, "Oh, where is my head, this is my new friend here, Zadkiel. You remember Zadkiel, don't you?"

I looked at the deer through my one eye, trying to ignore the unbearable pain. I didn't say anything.

"You northern boys have no manners. No hello? You don't recognize him? Come on, sport. What's the matter, Louie? You a little distracted? Difficult to think clearly? I thought you were the Animal

Killer. A real professional. It appears when the going gets tough, the Animal Killer, well, he crumbles. Zadkiel here, he's the deer you murdered shortly before you joined our little party. Zadkiel and I have been thinking up some real good ways to make sure you get your justice. Wouldn't be fair to short change you before we turn you over to that thing on the other side of that wall. Besides, that's all you really want, right Louie, justice? That's all any of us can really ask for at this point," he stated, looking me in my one good eye.

My anger for the Sport Hunter boiled. I lost another chance to throw myself at the Destroyer. I looked, but wasn't certain this was the same deer I had killed right before my death. My face became flush and my heartbeat hastened. I sucked in air a little harder and they looked at me. He did look a lot like him. I tried to remember. The grinning deer racing me through the clouds. *Did this mean my torment was possibly ending? Once this deer got his pound of flesh, his revenge?*

Azrael turned to another platoon of apes,

"Drag him back and nail him up to think about it some more. Get ready, Louie. The real fun is *gonna* start soon."

B. Lee Baker

Part 3

But if you do not forgive others, your Father will not forgive you your sins.

–Matthew 6:15 NET

B. Lee Baker

The Fourteenth Chapter

They dragged me back and again impaled me to the crucifix. They violently removed the arrows still imbedded in me, twisting and turning them before yanking them out. I turned to curse the Sport Hunter, but he wasn't there. The sign identifying him was gone as well.

"Where is he?" I asked, still looking at his cross.

The apes snickered. "Oh, he's gone. Won't be seeing him no more."

They turned and faded into the trees. I was now completely alone. Abandoned by God, and all that is good, left to suffer until completely destroyed. I sank into a pit of blackness.

"Why me?" I cried out.

It was an unheard question. Waves of doubt, sadness and loss washed over me like the tide moving in and out of a great ocean. Then, the most intense scenes from the Decider's *review* flashed in my mind's eye, plainly answering, why me. I was again forced to witness the suffering I had inflicted over the course of my life and I finally grasped the magnitude of what I had done. This shattered my arrogance and informed my ignorance. I could no longer hold the weight of my head and it dropped, driving my chin hard against my chest. The force propelled my body forward and tugged at the spikes imprisoning me. My psyche cracked and crashed, repaired and then cracked and crashed again. All the deaths I caused. The pain. The broken hearts. The screams and thoughts of all I had destroyed echoed in the chambers of my mind. I heard all the cries, and the anguish, as if it were playing out before me in real-time. All of it wove deeply into the fabric of my soul. Before my death, I had never considered any of it. Since my death, I haven't been allowed to think of anything else. My heart sank as I came to a conclusion that was hard to accept. I was the bad guy. I had never considered myself a bad guy. No one ever admits to anyone, not even to themselves, that they are the bad guy. But, in a world filled with bad guys, and failures and shortcomings, it was clear, the biggest lies we tell, are the ones we tell ourselves. Yes, I went to church. Yes, I tried to do right. Yes, I loved my family, but the lessons I've learned in death all point to this one inescapable conclusion.

Animal Killer

The light faded and an artificial dark coated this battlefield of butchery, a forced darkness.

"*Aughhh!*" Exploded, breaking the dark filled silence.

The wail erupted from behind the wall. It continued and increased in intensity, wrestling me away from my gloom, replacing it with terror. It was a harrowing spectacle. The squeals were the first sounds I heard from behind the wall. The thrashing and screaming continued for what felt like hours. I tried to shut my ears, but it was impossible. I wasn't certain, but surmised that the screams were the sounds of the destruction of what remained of the Sport Hunter. Proof, that what lie beyond that wall, was the Devil's factory, fulfilling its purpose of destroying those castaway by God. I didn't understand how the Sport Hunter held on for so long. *What could that thing be doing to him?* I reminded myself this was not the murder of a body, but the destruction of a soul created by God. The torture and suffering Azrael visited upon me was unthinkable. I couldn't imagine what could be worse, but the cries shouting out, sounded worse. I returned to my plan, presenting myself for destruction might not be the finest idea. My alternatives brought about more sorrow, because there were none. There was no escape from the torment. No place to turn. How could I willingly present myself for annihilation? I lamented and lifted my head towards the sky,

"Please. I beg you. Take your foot off my throat. I am sorry. At some point there must be mercy. Just end it. I don't want to be here anymore. Just end it!" I shouted.

Shortly after my death, I had been so excited to learn the secrets of the world. Now, I just wanted it to end. I no longer wanted to fight or to figure things out or a way to escape. I just wanted it done. I had no idea how to set things right. A sudden blinding flash lit up the sky. The illumination was so bright it was as if the sun itself exploded. The blast hurt, temporarily blinding me. The screaming immediately stopped and silence enveloped the world. I assumed I just heard the obliteration of the Sport Hunter's soul. I never even knew his story, or his crime, but, his given name revealed much. I feared that would be how I would sound when my time came. I had no idea if his family continued to live and mourn his passing on Earth, or had passed themselves, as he feared. Were they searching for his soul to join them in Heaven? Two things seemed certain. He was gone, and, I was next. I prayed for Joey, the Sport Hunter, as he requested. It was a simple, but heartfelt prayer,

"God. Have mercy on him. Whatever his crime. Let him rest now."

Animal Killer

There would be no one to pray for me after I was destroyed. Only by the grace of God would I, could I, be saved. And, that didn't seem likely. God didn't exist in this place. God doesn't visit Hell. This was the place where He cast off the unwanteds and undesirables, not the place He came to save. I was most assuredly alone.

A twig cracked, tearing me from my dejected morose thoughts. I looked up and watched a deer slowly make his way toward me. He was injured and moved with a limp. He was alone and paused every few steps to look around. An unseen squawking owl shattered the silence, paralyzing him. I wouldn't swear to it, but I believe he swallowed hard. With all I had been through, and all the damage, I no longer trusted my senses. I couldn't distinguish between what was real, and what was not. The hidden screeching owl quieted and took off from the tree top, his thrashing wings exposing his departure. The deer looked around and continued his approach. A tree branch, still grasping its leaves, broke free and fell, hitting the ground causing the buck to leap off the ground. I watched and wondered, *what was this about?* This was something different. Not another attack, I wishfully reasoned. This deer seemed way too skittish to attack. I had to be dreaming.

The deer moved closer. I was then able to recognize it was in fact the deer I had murdered moments before my death. The one who accompanied me on the ride through the sky to Hell. He was here for his revenge. I uncontrollably peed down my leg. I was wrong, it was the next attack. The smiling deer had finally come for his revenge.

I whimpered,

"No. No more. I don't want this anymore. I don't care what I did. Enough. Please. I am sorry. I really am. I've suffered enough."

"*Shhhhhh.*" He whispered. "You want to get us killed?"

"Yes. Yes I do actually. True death is all I pray for."

"*Pff,* man, you don't mean that. You have no idea. Death doesn't mean what you think it does in this place. You have no clue what really goes on behind that wall. You think what Azrael does is bad? It *ain't* nothing compared to that. And that's exactly where they'll send your dumbass if we're caught. I'll be cannibalized, and your ass will be annihilated. Now shut up and take it easy. Don't make me regret this."

Since arriving in this place of perdition, I have experienced nothing but cruelty and indifference. I didn't know how to process or react.

"If I get your ass down, you're not going to attack me, are you? I'm not one of them."

"Attack you?" I was confounded.

"Yeah. Hurt me. You know– try to kill me. Given your past, it's not a crazy question. You and I both know you have a long history of abusing my kind. Sign hanging right there above your head calls you the Animal Killer. So you'll have to forgive me for asking."

"No. I won't hurt you. Please, I just want to get down." I wavered between believing this was real and some sort of hallucination or a trick.

He looked me in the eyes for a moment, not moving.

"Guess, that'll have to do."

He stepped to my side and murmured to himself,

"I shouldn't even be here. What are you doing, Zadkiel? You must have lost your mind. Putting your own ass on the line like this."

He then turned to me.

"When I've got you free, follow me and move fast. No talking."

I nodded my head the best I could. I was in shock. The deer opened his mouth and clamped down with his teeth, grabbing the steel spike pinning my right wrist to my cross. Before he removed it, he whispered with the spike still in his mouth,

"Not a word. All hell's *gonna* break loose."

He then yanked the spike from the cross and spit it out onto the ground. The moment it was free, a horn began to wail. It buzzed from all directions, raining down from the sky above and even from the earth below. He then quickly removed the spike from my right leg. With my left wrist and leg still pinned to the cross, my body involuntarily swung to the left. The way a door swings open. I held onto the left side of the crucifix. The deer leapt to my left and tore out the remaining spikes. As he removed each, the constant crushing pain and dread subsided. Once the last spike was removed, I fell to the ground. I slowly stood, in disbelief. I was free. *Was this really happening?*

"Let's go." He commanded.

I stood there immobilized and stunned. The ground began to tremble and the horn continued to blare.

He looked back and saw me frozen, standing and staring at him.

"Jesus. Come on, man. We got to get out of here. Right now! There's no time to think! For God's sake! Freaking humans, cannot follow simple instructions. And, I'm the dumb animal?"

Animal Killer

I had no idea if I could trust this animal, but the fact he didn't attack me while I was prone and helpless revealed much. Anything different than another attack or hunt was welcomed. I decided to embrace it and followed him. He picked up the pace when the ground shook. The horn betraying my escape continued to sound. The shaking earth announced Azrael and his army knew I had been freed. They were on the move and heading our way.

I raced and zig zagged through the landscape trying to keep up with this deer. We both were singularly focused on putting as much distance between us and the rumbling advancing squad of vengeful animals. Every so often he turned to make sure I was still behind him.

"Come on, keep up." He whispered, annoyed.

We journeyed for a very long time. The horns faded in the distance. Now, there wasn't a sound. Not a cricket. Nothing. Just a barren wasteland, but for the two of us. The fleeing felons. Free from my bondage, my wounds again started to heal. I began slowly to regain my strength and my sick suffering eased bit by bit. My will to go on sluggishly returned. I didn't know what that meant. To go on. What would that look like in this place or where? My craving for food and water and my constant chill firmly remained, relentlessly taunting me. We headed toward a very large snowcapped mountain range. I couldn't tolerate the silence. I continued to contemplatively question why this animal would help me. I killed him. I had so many questions. I settled on something simple, to feel him out.

"What's that limp about?" I motioned my head.

"Oh yeah, well . . . call that an old war wound. Let's save the chit chat for now. I *ain't* getting caught on account of your dumbass questions."

He wasn't ready to talk, so I went on autopilot and followed him. I watched him masterfully traverse the terrain despite the limp. I didn't know what to make of all of this. I was immensely grateful to be off the cross. Immeasurably thankful he was helping me. I just had such a hard time understanding how someone, or rather how some thing, could be that forgiving. I tried to calculate his possible ulterior motives. Before I knew it, I found myself in familiar surroundings. I had not been paying attention.

"Wait! . . . wait." I whispered.

The deer stopped.

"What now?"

"I was told to never to go that way."

We were heading toward the place Joey had told me to never go.

"Uh huh. And who told you that?"

"Joey."

"Who the hell is, Joey?"

"The, Sport Hunter, the guy hanging next to me."

"Look, don't worry about it. I don't know Joey. He *ain't* my problem. That' just some crazy shit they tell to scare away dumbasses like you. To keep you out. They *really* don't want you coming here."

"Why not?"

"Because even crazy bastards have their threshold for tolerating discomfort."

"Why, what's so bad about this place?"

"You sure do ask a lot of questions for a man teetering between suicide and extinction. It's where they bury their secrets, so they avoid coming here. That's why it's the perfect place to hide out. Okay? We about done with the *Q* and *A*?"

I didn't force it, he would tell me when, and if, I needed to know. He pressed on and I followed. I continued to be in awe at how well he navigated the mountainous terrain. He skillfully maneuvered down the side of the steep mountain. I clumsily tumbled and slid down after him. Every so often he glanced back at me with a disapproving look. The bottom led us to a wide valley. Ahead in the distance I saw a black wrought iron fence that marked the entranceway to a large dry basin. It looked like the entrance to an old cemetery in a horror movie.

After what felt like forever, the deer finally broke his silence, twisting his neck and head around to face me.

"No *freakin* out."

"Freak out? Why would . . . I . . . freak . . . ou–" I slowed my pace, as my words hung in the air unfinished.

At first, I wasn't sure what I was seeing. The mind is a trick master. Particularly when you force it to process a ghastly scene. It simultaneously will understand exactly what stands before it, while at the same time it will erect a wall, protecting it from comprehending a grotesque, upsetting scene. As we got closer, that protective wall crumbled and I gasped. My hand involuntarily shot to my mouth as I sucked in my next breath. Hard. It was an unfamiliar sound to me. Thousands, maybe more, of bodies hung from the trees. A mass lynching. A massacre of biblical proportions. When we got to the gate, I understood they weren't human carcasses at all, but rather the torsos of very large dead rams that hung from the dry bare trees. Someone, or some thing, tied nooses around their necks and strung them up from the tree branches. Their horns had been sawed off. Every single one of them. But none of the dangling flaccid cadavers were decomposing. It was a permeant testament to the genocide. We maneuvered cautiously through the maze of hanging corpses. I did my best not to touch them, but it was difficult, there were so many. Each time either of us accidently bumped into one, it set off a chain reaction, like the metal tubes of a wind chime colliding. Instead of emitting pleasant soothing tones, it set off the cascading sick sound of the thud of dead flesh slapping against other dead flesh. It was a terrifying sight and mortifying sound.

"What is this place?" I asked in a whisper.

"They killed them all and brought them here to hang. They kill them still. But now there is only one left. At least only one they know about. More will come. Then the last one. This is why they will come here last. It's a reminder of how they betray their own. It reminds them of what they really are. So this makes it the safest place for you, and me."

"Look, this is nuts. I've got to know. Why are you helping me?"

"That is a very good question. Call me stupid or crazy. Maybe both. Risking getting myself killed for you, doesn't make much sense. One thing I do know, you should be grateful my friend."

I lowered my head. Embarrassed.

"I'm sorry." I offered.

"For what? Asking too many questions? Walking too slow? Killing me? I should be torturing your dumb ass. Not saving it."

We continued to walk in silence for a bit. I wasn't sure what to say, but I was grateful.

Finally, I tried again, "I'm sorry, I don't remember your name. I am still getting used to you animals being able to speak and having names. Something like, Zedka?"

"You animals? What in hell do you mean– *you* animals? And you're surprised we can talk? We communicate all the time. Your dumbass just never could figure out our languages. Good thing too, you would have just used it to enslave or kill more of us. And why wouldn't I have a name? You think my friends and family call me deer? I suppose we all look the same to you also, huh?"

I laughed. I tried to suppress it, which only made it sound that much worse. I couldn't help myself.

"What the hell is so funny?"

"Nothing. I'm sorry."

"My name is Zadkiel. And I'll call you dumbass. Seems rather fitting under the circumstances. Keep pissing me off and I'll be calling you dead dumbass. I'm guessing my name doesn't sound familiar to you, does it?"

"Should I recognize it?"

He shook his head in disapproval.

"You know, every time you open your pie hole I regret helping you. It's no freaking big mystery why you're here."

No matter how insulting he was, I could not get angry with him. We continued to travel deeper into the valley of the slaughtered rams. Except for the clatter of our steps, there was not a sound. A thought raced to the forefront of my mind. *Was he leading me further toward Oblivion? Was this his opportunity for revenge? Why would he help me*, I wondered. I dismissed the concern. The Spirit Destroyer was far behind us, and that was fine by me.

"Tell me about the limp."

"Why are you so concerned?"

"It just seems out of the ordinary in this place."

"Yea, well this place *ain't* the same for all of us. But, since you're so interested, I can still feel where you shot me. A little present from the powers that be. A constant reminder of why I should be killing your ass, rather than saving it. Happy you asked?"

I turned red. Shame overwhelmed me.

B. Lee Baker

The Fifteenth Chapter

U pon learning he still suffered because of me, my shame grew and found it even more remarkable that this animal risked his life to help me. I waited for the ulterior motive to emerge, the punchline to reveal itself. In my experience, there was little, if any, forgiveness in the real world. Not really. Only when those who refuse to forgive, transgress themselves, then they freely offer it and plead for it in return, unable to find it. Instead, conflict was settled by Judges, not forgiveness, and then, only after a raucous war, waged with the lethal weapons of words and paper. Forgiveness came in a distant fourth place behind hyperbole, anger and revenge. I had such little experience with forgiveness, it was hard to accept. I knew it best as a word and theoretical concept, not a reality to be practiced. Even in my personal life, battle lines were quickly and frequently drawn. Anyone who dared to cross me received my wrath and retribution. And after my death, neither the

Deciders nor Azrael showed any forgiveness. Yet, this deer, whom I executed, freely offered it to me.

A faint foreign cry broke the silence. We both froze and looked at one another.

"What the hell is that?" I asked.

"Oh, man. My luck cannot be this bad."

"What?"

"The missing baby lamb Azrael has been hunting. He'll kill her if he finds her. It's the only thing that has him distracted from focusing on you full time. We have to find her."

"Hold on. Let's think about this. Is that such a good idea? What's so important about this lamb? Shouldn't we prioritize here? I'm in agony over here. I'm really hungry, thirsty and cold. Maybe we can address those first and make sure we're safe before we go heading off on a rescue mission."

"You see– It's that kind of thinking that's going to make me regret helping you. You're still the same selfish person you've been your whole life. I should just leave your ass and go find her myself."

"No! No, you're right. I'm sorry."

He was right. Old habits die hard.

"Unbelievable! You have no idea how lucky you are."

"Lucky? I don't feel very lucky."

"You know, today was your day. You were done. Azrael was taking your ass to the Destroyer, you know, the executioner of souls, or whatever crazy bad ass name they've been calling that thing."

"Not true. Azrael said I was going to be around here for a long time."

"Oh, yes, it is true my friend. You were going to roast. Today. As much as a day has meaning in this place. Azrael loves talking crazy. It's his way of waging psychological warfare. He just says stuff like that to terrify and demoralize you. He thinks it makes him a bigger badass."

"Then Karma lied to me. He told me I'd see him again. I thought I was getting a second chance. This is no chance."

"I don't know about any of that. I just know you were going through those doors, today. So a little appreciation and cooperation are in order. Now help me look for this lamb. And, one more thing– stop your whining about your hunger and thirst, the constant complaining about being cold! It's getting old, you don't need to worry about any of that here. You'd be deader than you're already dead if you did. Man– what was God thinking when He put you at the top of the food chain? You're really some kind of slow. No wonder the world is screwed up. He should have put us deer in charge. Then you'd see some shit get done."

I knew he was right. While time had no meaning in this place, given all that has happened I would be gone by now. I had not eaten since my death and haven't had any water since I first got here, and yet, here I am. I still didn't understand what I was feeling.

"So why do I feel the way I do?"

He moved in the direction of the cries that had since stopped. I followed.

"You only think you feel thirst and hunger and cold. These are residue sensations of your former life. In this place, the physical body doesn't need food, water or heat. The soul doesn't have the same needs as the physical body. I cannot believe not only do I have to rescue your sorry ass, but I've got to teach you the things you should already know or figured out for yourself."

"I'm sorry."

"Stop apologizing. It's annoying."

It was getting a little pathetic. But I was a broken man, battered and destroyed. He stopped moving and looked at me.

"I'll try to speak plain. You're obviously slow. Are all humans as slow as you? The sensations you're experiencing are the cravings of your soul. Like your body on Earth, the soul requires certain things to survive. Those things are just as critical as food, water, and warmth. What you're feeling now is your soul crying out to you, because you withhold what it needs to survive. When it is denied, you experience sensations similar to depriving yourself of food or water or warmth. You are just interpreting these things as hunger, thirst and cold. When alive, most people unconsciously feed the soul paltry fragments of the things it needs to thrive. They instead focus on the needs of the flesh and ignore the needs of the soul. Life lived this way results in the soul receiving, by default, just enough to survive. The angst and depression and dread and negative feelings people experience are all manifestations of the depravation of what the soul needs to survive. People try to feed it food, water, alcohol, drugs, they try to fill themselves with the stuff they buy. But all that just masks the basic cravings of the soul. Here, you're nothing but soul."

"Jesus."

"No, Zadkiel."

"Huh?" I questioned.

"You called me Jesus. Name is Zadkiel."

"Funny. Okay, Zadkiel. Are you going to tell me what my soul needs so I can start feeling better?"

He paused, giving me a long, serious look before answering.

"Your soul needs to live by the word of the Creator. The word is the food for the soul. Without it, the soul starves and hungers. This feeling cannot be satisfied with food. Eat all the food you want, your soul will continue to hunger. If you gain all the riches and wealth of the world, you'll continue to remain hungry, empty. You don't meditate on the word of God. And, even more important, you do not live by the word of God. You deny it. Ignore it. You still refuse to understand and accept the word of God since your death and, thus, you hunger. The soul cannot live without this food. This is why with each passing moment in this place, you lose hope. You lose the will to go on. Your life force is dying. You are starving, just not the way you thought you are. Understand?

I said nothing. Instead, I contemplated how he had just pulled back the curtain, revealing a great mystery that had escaped me all my life.

"You didn't get this when you went to church every week? Unbelievable."

"I– I didn't . . ."

"Oh, now you're at loss for words. Your soul also craves righteousness and justice. This is what you are experiencing as thirst. It seeks justice for itself, and justice for all. Your soul is being denied righteousness and justice. Without it, the soul thirsts. It cannot be quenched by water. Drink all the water you want, you will still thirst. You haven't fought for justice, haven't given justice. Worse still, you fail to repent for denying it to so many. The soul cannot live without this water. Without it, your soul dehydrates, dries up and dies. Got it?

I nodded. Astonished. So simple, and yet so elusive. He turned and continued heading deeper into the valley. I followed.

"And the constant cold I feel?"

"Your soul needs to give and to receive love. The lack of love is what you experience as cold. You have not been loved since arriving here. You have been cut off from God. Cut off from the family who loved you. You have not offered love to anyone since you arrived here. Without receiving and freely spreading love, the soul freezes in the abyss. The soul cannot live without the warm comfort of love. It cannot be warmed by fire. Burn all the wood you want, you will still freeze. Without all of these things your soul will die. You are dying, Louie. Similar to the death you experience when you deny your earthly body food to eat, water to drink, or fire for warmth, you suffer spiritual death when you deny yourself these most important things. This is the worst possible death. This place was an opportunity for you to supply these things to your soul through your deeds and thoughts. Instead, you've angered and dismissed those you've wronged. You've hardened your heart. You've resisted embracing a change of heart, holding on to your corrupt beliefs, so your soul cools, as you head toward the abyss."

"I didn't know. I wish I had."

"The truth is your soul needed these things when you lived. Your soul was dying long before you arrived here. Had you been concerned with feeding your spirit, you would not be where you are now. But instead, you satisfied and fulfilled your own selfish desires, filling your mind, your body, with all the trappings of the material world. All the wrong stuff. Dead animals for food. Dead animals for trophies. Shinny material possessions that all fade away. You failed to see there is nothing the human can offer as an adequate substitute for what the Big Man offers. You deny yourself the word of God, the true food that it needs. Without the word everything else falls. You lose the quest for righteousness and create a world less and less just. This in turn creates a world filled with less and less love. When justice is denied for one, it is denied for all. When you are unrighteous, you are denied righteousness. When you are denied righteousness you deprive your soul the true drink it needs to satisfy your thirst. When you refuse to accept love, when you withhold love, your soul in turn is not loved. When you do not receive love, your soul is not given the true warmth it needs to remain alive."

Animal Killer

A faint wail cried off in the distance and Zadkiel turned and darted in that direction. I followed.

"Thank you. I understand."

I was numb. The true and holy meaning of life had just been revealed to me. I sadly understood I lived a life so far from its purpose.

"Do you? I hope so my friend. Because, even if we somehow manage to avoid being captured by that crazy elk hunting your ass, what's left of your wasted life will depend on it. You want to know why I am here? I am here to give you a message," he stopped to look at me to make sure I would hear him clearly, and that it was as important as anything he had said. "Repent. Repent for your sins. Repent for your ignorance. Repent for living a selfish life. Repent for the cruelty and indifference, for not offering mercy. Repent for not loving more, for not loving everyone and every thing God created."

I raised my hand to remove my matted, dirty hair from my eyes. Zadkiel leapt back three feet, startled.

"Still don't trust me?" I asked sadly.

"Would you if you were me? I mean fool me once shame on you, fool me twice and I am going after the *sonofabitch*. Something like that is how the saying goes."

"It was an accident." I told him.

"Come again?"

"Shooting you. It was an accident."

"Did you not hear a single word I just said? You must think I'm a goddamn fool." He shouted. "Man, now look what you made me do, taking the Lord's name in vain. I've been working on that. I should deliver your sorry ass myself to that beast behind the wall. They're no secrets here, Louie. I know what you did and exactly why you did it. Everyone does. And most important for you, God and Azrael know. God isn't listening now, and Azrael won't stop until you pay the ultimate price for what you've done."

I looked down. My face flushed and warm with embarrassment.

"The reason I'm helping your dumbass is I'd like to believe you're better than the life you lived. I want to believe you weren't born the Animal Killer, but that you were taught to be the Animal Killer, but I'm just not sure."

I continued looking down.

"I want to believe deep down in that thick skull of yours, you feel it too. Not because of Saint Francis and the judgment of the Deciders. But, because deep down, you know the truth. You were made to protect them, not slaughter them. To love your neighbor. And, your neighbor is the community of the world, and everything in it. You were led astray. Led by the evil one, who first corrupts and distorts, and then stays alive by feasting on the souls of lost men like you. I'd like to believe you're ready to stop being a fool, but to be completely honest, I am helping you for me. You see, my dead ass is here for a reason too. I should be *kickin* it in Heaven right now, floating on the clouds or whatever super cool crazy shit that goes on there. But, I was filled with rage. I too wanted revenge. It's only natural, right? I was given the choice. Seek revenge, or forgive. I am choosing to forgive."

"I don't know what to say to all of that. Thank you. I am not sure I could forgive as easily as you. I am actually sure I couldn't, wouldn't," I admitted, shifting and fidgeting.

"Yeah. Well. That's why your ass has been getting obliterated bit by bit. That's why you suffer. That's why you're hungry, thirsty and cold. Choice is yours. Always has been. Every day is a new day. You get to wake up and decide what kind of man you want to be. Doesn't matter what you did yesterday. Doesn't matter what anyone else says or expects from you."

"And what about all these animals?"

"What about them?"

"They don't seem to be living by the word or giving justice or love. Why are they here? What happens to them?"

"Yeah. Well– again their purpose here is different than yours. Same rules don't apply. God works in mysterious ways. Animals can die here, humans don't, except on the other side of that wall. Some of these animals have been here for a very long time. They are stuck. Some were wronged and can't give up the desire for revenge. Some were humans seeking revenge, but now are forced to live as animals. God is a clever *mothereffing* master. In the same place, He is giving everyone a chance to be what they should. To let go what they need to let go. To give what they want to receive."

"And you chose to forgive?"

"That's right. I choose to forgive. I did some bad stuff in my past. How can I ask for forgiveness if I won't forgive? I've learned my lessons. Will you? Pretty simple if you think about it, you know, do unto others . . . as you were commanded. Probably would have only taken you a few thousand years to figure all this out."

Part 4

Do not be conformed to this present world, but be transformed by the renewing of your mind, so that you may test and approve what is the will of God – what is good and well-pleasing and perfect.

–Romans 12:2 NET

B. Lee Baker

The Sixteenth Chapter

The cries and bleats resumed and grew louder. Zadkiel and I shot a panicked look at one another. The sound would undoubtedly attract Azrael and his wrath. We had to quickly find this lamb. I was, however, grateful for the distraction from my deepening shame. In the quietness and seclusion of this landscape littered with the remains of a mass slaughter, my thoughts gnawed at me. In these moments, free from Azrael's torture, my mind repeatedly returned to the lessons and teachings offered to me since my death. I could no longer view the hanging corpses with passive indifference. I had to look away. I wondered how the remains of the ones I had slaughtered throughout my lifetime would look were they to line them up and hang them from trees. Despite my subconscious' best effort to hide it, I now understand the magnitude of what I had done. The families I tore apart. The pain I had inflicted. The damage done to the unseen fabric woven by God that ties all of His creations together. The damage I had done to countless others, myself, and most importantly, God. I was condemned, and my suffering just. My offenses were horrific. My only defense was that I was blind. I was arrogant and ignorant.

"Wipe that frown off your face." Zadkiel barked. "You can feel sorry for yourself later. If we don't get those cries to stop, Azrael will find us and toast both our asses."

"Why'd they kill all these rams?" I asked.

"That's one thing you don't have to worry about . . . I don't think." He turned away.

I was going to press him, but we finally located the crying baby lamb. She was no bigger than an average house cat. I guessed she weighed ten pounds, at most. She was covered in a pristine brilliant white coat of fleece. She quivered with fear. An involuntary reaction I had never felt before, sprung from deep within me. I felt for her. It happened just like that. She was alone amidst a slaughter of her kind. She looked frightened, not knowing what we might do to her. She was powerless and at the mercy of whatever, or whoever, came upon her. It was the first time I had ever felt for an animal.

"Pick her up. We have to move deeper into this valley," Zadkiel instructed.

"Pick her up?" I repeated. "Are you joking?"

"Do I sound like I'm joking? Do I seem jokey to you?"

"I'd rather not. I don't even know how."

"Look, Louie, do I look like I can pick her up? You need to pick her up and get her to stop that bleating or crying, whatever that is she's doing. And we need to keep moving."

The lamb brushed up against my leg.

"Louie, pick her up. This is Moriah."

"How do you know her name?"

"I told you, Azrael has been looking for her. This is all they've been talking about."

"Why her? I thought he had been killing rams."

"I was told about her before I got here. Azrael doesn't take any chances. He likes to get them while they are young, before they can procreate."

"I still don't understand. She's not a ram."

Zadkiel closed his eyes and shook his head.

"Louie . . . I don't know what to say. I do feel sorry for you. I have no doubt you fattened yourself on several servings of lamb."

"I've eaten a few legs of lamb in my day, if that's what you're asking." I blurted out, regretting I admitted it the moment I said it.

"Pitiful," he barked shaking his head. "And you never took the time to know anything about them. Never appreciated the sacrifice they made. Well, surprise, Louie, a ram is an adult male lamb or sheep, as they are also known. I'm going to assume you were absent from school the day they taught . . . I don't know . . . everything!"

I shrugged. "Hey, how about that. I never knew that."

"Yea how about that. School is in session. Can we please get going now?"

"Can she speak?"

"Don't know for sure. She can't or won't. She has been on her own since she got here. She isn't like the rest of us. Innocent as they get. Unblemished. They told me she was sent to be a sacrifice for you. But that it would be your choice."

"Wait. What? What do you mean, a sacrifice?"

"The Deciders. They told me they would send her here. They told me you could offer her to Azrael, to take your place. Handing her over will end your suffering."

"What– that doesn't make any sense."

"What makes sense? The Creator's ways are not our ways."

More than anything, I wanted this over. Moriah started to cry again. She could be my way out of this hell. I knelt down next to her and began to pet her. It felt uncomfortable and unnatural to me.

"Come on. No crying," I ordered. "You're going to get all of us caught if you keep that up."

She flopped down to the ground and on to her side like she had become paralyzed from my touch. She then made a weird sound, similar to a cat's purr, a soft bleat. Her tongue protruded slightly from her smiling mouth.

I looked at Zadkiel.

"Well, at least she stopped crying." I said proudly.

"You hear that, Louie? That's the sound of God."

"Sound of God?"

"God reveals himself. We just need to look and listen for Him. If you want to hear the sound of God, just listen. You can hear it in every being. Listen to a cat purr. Watch a dog wag its tail. Listen to a child laugh. These are all expressions of God. Now, pick her ass up and let's move!"

I pushed away my discomfort and scooped her up. She instantly relaxed and became completely docile in my arms. I flipped her over and cradled her like a baby. Her legs pointed up, but then slowly relaxed bending downward. She looked into my eyes and continued to make this sound of contentment. The sound of God. I continued to move forward with my attention firmly on her. She looked fake and felt like a little child's stuffed animal. The chill that had been stalking me began to wane. My cold body warmed for the first time since arriving here. Initially, I wanted to believe that it was this little white sack of fluff that was giving off the warming heat. She reminded me of a giant marshmallow. But now I understood, it was love. Grateful, I suddenly felt indebted to her.

I hadn't noticed Zadkiel stopped walking, and watched me, watch her in my arms.

"What are you smiling at?" He asked.

I didn't realize I was smiling. I stopped walking, still cradling Moriah.

"I don't know. I just feel different."

I experienced an odd sensation. The invisible shackles of my ignorance that unconsciously imprisoned me, unlocked and fell, releasing me, unleashing love that had been bound and contained. The feeling cascaded through me, bringing about the beginning of a profound change. But as nice as it felt, I impulsively resisted and fought it.

"Imagine that, Louie. You show a little kindness, and look what it does. Proof, you don't have to be the same dumbass you were yesterday. Every day starts anew, it doesn't matter what you've been taught, or believed before, or even what you did in the past. Every day, you get to choose who to be."

Zadkiel turned his gaze away from me and resumed onward, offering one last slice of sage advice, "Now you know, you can be the light in the midst of the darkness, or not. It's up to you."

I wondered, how I could possibly be a light. It didn't matter what I've learned, what I would do, or the price I have paid, I was headed to Oblivion for all I had done. But, I did know, that I could follow the word and live a life of righteousness until my last breath.

We walked deeper into the valley of the rams. The quietness was all consuming. There was nothing here. Just the three of us as we moved deeper into what was a mass grave. Then we met a large dilapidated barn. The red paint had peeled and faded, turning brown.

"Looks like a good place to holed up." Zadkiel said.

I put Moriah down so I could swing open the oversized door. She immediately started to bleat again and rub up against my legs.

"Alright. Alright. One minute." I said to her.

Zadkiel stepped inside and Moriah and I followed. There was nothing inside, but large piles of straw. I had never seen anything look so good. I leapt into the air, my abrupt maneuver startling them both. They tensed, readied to take flight. They both still feared the Animal Killer. Who could blame them? But if this place accomplished nothing else, it eradicated the Animal Killer. They had nothing to fear from me. I landed, sharply, in a thick bed of straw, the dry stray strands stabbing at me. Once I settled in, however, it was glorious, the first serene moment that allowed me to reflect and consider all that had happened. They finally relaxed when they saw I was enjoying myself. I closed my eyes and almost instantly felt refreshed. The memories of the coliseum and chants from the millions of animals asking for justice seemed so far away. My perpetual crucifixion and Azrael's ruthless army was far away. I was free.

Moriah followed my lead and took flight jumping squarely onto my stomach shattering my peace. I gasped from the unexpected blow even though she was a mere ten pounds or so. Moriah remained half on my stomach, half on my chest, her face inches from mine. She positioned herself so her legs folded beneath her. She looked like a hen sitting on an egg. She stared into my eyes with a look of contentment and resumed her catlike purr.

"What are you doing?" I asked. "I need to rest. Go sit over there." I pointed toward Zadkiel.

"She likes your sorry ass. Don't know why, but she does."

"What does she want from me?"

"She's been alone for a long time. I assume she's happy to have a friend. Even if it is you."

"What am I supposed to do?"

"I don't know. Be nice. Be kind. Try petting her. Make her feel safe. Jesus Christ! Can you believe I have to teach the human how to be human? You'd better figure out what she likes because we need to keep her quiet or we're all going to get caught. I am going to rest and think about what we should do next."

I stroked the top of her head with my thumb. I moved it between her eyes and down the bridge of her nose, in long gentle strokes. I also massaged her spine. Her eyes continued to gaze into mine as she began to fall asleep. I couldn't believe I was petting a baby lamb. In my prior life, I would have been thinking about how to prepare her for dinner. But I had to admit, it actually felt– nice. The warmth washed over me. I digested Zadkiel's words, amazed that this tough talking deer was actually filled with remarkable wisdom. Every day could be a new start. We don't have to be inflicted with the consequences of yesterday or the inertia of life. My anger with myself deepened as I considered all the church services I had attended and ignored. Why did I bother to go? I never learned the word. Never lived it. Never really loved. I realized I was exactly where I belonged, but that didn't make any of this easier to accept.

We both fell asleep lying exactly as we were.

The ensuing visions I experienced could not be more real. I relived my death. My son standing over me. Zadkiel dead next to me. Me shouting to the heavens, *who's the man!* I looked down at Zadkiel dead on the frozen Earth. The same deer who has now rescued me from Azrael and the Spirit Destroyer. I watched God create the world. This time, unlike the painted moving picture I previously saw, I watched God breathe life into every living being. The God of creation was magnificent. The emanating light so bright, He was impossible to stare at for more than a moment. His lips slightly parted as I watched a white light leave His mouth and enter the mouth and nostrils of being after being. Human and animal alike. The breath of life. It was part of His soul that poured into every thing. And then I watched myself stomp and kill and maim them. Killing and assaulting God with each unspeakable act. How could I expect anything from Him? I had not repented for these sins. I had destroyed Him for no other purpose but to showoff to my colleagues and friends. I tormented a woman on the internet who had done nothing wrong, but call me out for being cruel and ungodly.

I had been stripped of everything. My life, my family, my ego, my control and my beliefs. I was left with only the weight of embarrassment and shame. The words of Karma and Saint Francis pinballed about in the chambers of my mind. I realized I was utterly ignorant of what it truly meant to be a Christian. I had wholly failed to abide by the command to love my neighbor in all the forms I found them. I finally understood why, no matter how hard I tried to catch him, God remained beyond my reach. Despite my apparent earthly successes of family and money, God remained a mystery to me. I had always hoped that God had turned from me for only a season and that He would one day return. I now understood. The truth was that I never moved toward Him. I ignored His word and will. I never tried to live the life He expected. I had never took the time to read the Bible, only brief passages when in church. Why is it that only after we lose everything, are our eyes opened?

I woke up and opened my eyes with a singular thought and realized that one way or another, we are all lambs headed toward the slaughter. Believe it or not. Understand it or not. I had been praying for God to end my agony without any willingness to repent for the agony I had caused. I asked for mercy without offering mercy to others. I asked for forgiveness, unwilling to forgive. I looked down and watched Moriah sleeping on top of me. I looked upon this little innocent creature and silently cried to the Creator like a wounded animal in the night. I begged for Him to return to me. For the first time, I understood she was as helpless as a human child. Both souls working their way through the world. She just wanted to be safe and loved and protected. She felt pain and hunger and neglect, just as any human. I understood not only had she been created by God, she was, in part, God Himself. To do anything to harm or neglect her was an affront to the Creator Himself. Why had this message been so lost on me? It seems so obvious now. We choose to be what we are. What to believe. What to ignore. Like sheep, we herd together to protect ourselves. We follow the flock and assume there is safety in the collective conscious. Some of us think of ourselves wolves, some sheepdogs and believe we are independent and strong. But, it's all an illusion. In the end, we are all sheep, and will fall upon on our knees before the face of God when He renders what we are due. We don't stop often enough to question whether we are being led to salvation or damnation.

I now have a new appreciation for those few brave souls who wander alone against all odds, in the face of ridicule, scorn and hostility and choose to follow the word of God and His will. They are the voices who cry out in the wilderness, pleading and showing how the rest of us should follow the righteous path. I decided in that moment, whether I had much, or little time remaining in this place or elsewhere, I would be a voice crying out for what is right and just in the wilderness, in Heaven, if I ever make it there, or back on Earth. I would scream it wherever and to whomever would listen to save them. I'll scream it to Azrael and his army. And, yes, I will shout it to the Spirit Destroyer when we meet.

B. Lee Baker

The Seventeenth Chapter

I turned and saw Zadkiel watching me. Our eyes locked. His expression warmed. His look conveyed that he understood. He felt the seismic shockwaves emanating from the profound conversion in my understanding. The tectonic shift that had taken place and would forever change me. My body softened and relaxed. I hadn't realized how tense it had been beforehand. A tension that probably existed all my life. Now, a peacefulness washed over me.

"I am so sorry." I said with sorrow, but with conviction, free from any reservation. It was distinctly different from the meek, obligatory apology I had previously offered to him. "I truly am. I am sorry I did that to you. It is . . . unforgiveable. All I can offer is that I didn't understand. I stole your life and caused you pain. Words cannot make amends. How can God forgive that? How can you? I am heading to Oblivion, and I deserve it."

"I don't know. You did some bad stuff, but I forgive your dumbass."

"How can you forgive me?"

"Already told you. I forgive because that is what the Big Man commands. If I want forgiveness for the bad I've done, I have to forgive you for the bad you've done to me. No getting around that."

I smiled at him, but my heart ached. Moriah woke. She stepped off me and stretched. Then she shook and twisted her whole body like a dog drying itself after getting wet. I smiled.

"Tell me. Why'd they kill all the rams? Why hang them? Why not bury or incinerate them? Why are they hunting Moriah?"

"Because Azrael is one crazy mother fucker. The rams were using their horns to batter down the doors, willing to sacrifice themselves to kill the Spirit Destroyer, or at least stop him from annihilating any more souls. They believed he'd choke on their horns. Azrael doesn't want that to happen. He hangs them because without burying them or cremating them, he thinks they cannot be resurrected to come back to try again. It leaves them in limbo."

"Why would they do that, sacrifice themselves? And, why does Azrael care?"

"Many of the rams were human. The Deciders sent them to this place in the form of a ram. They had done their own evil and owed a debt to God. It was their way to repent. They believed if they killed the Spirit Destroyer they would regain God's grace. But, when the Big Man is ready, He'll send the one lamb that will end this and there won't be a thing Azrael, or anyone else, will be able to do to stop it."

"Sorry. I still don't get it. Why kill the lambs?"

"'Then the kings of the earth, the princes, the generals, the rich, the mighty, and everyone else, both slave and free, hid in caves and among the rocks of the mountains. They called to the mountains and the rocks, fall on us and hide us from the face of him who sits on the throne and from the wrath of the Lamb!'"

He saw my perplexed look.

"Revelation, Louie. The wrath of the lamb."

My blank stare persisted.

"Jesus H. Christ. How can one man spend so much time going to church and not have learned a damn thing? I guess you figured you were baptized, gave a few dollars when the collection plate was passed around, and that meant you were good to go. Unbelievable! I'm talking about the end of time! When God will once and for all end this. The prophesy states the sinners will try to run and hide from the wrath of the lamb."

"I don't understand. If the animals are victims, what are they so worried about, why would Azrael delay the wrath of the lamb, I'd think he would welcome it? Why fight against God?"

"I told you. Not all the animals are victims. Many were former humans who lived wicked lives, sent here to experience their offenses from a different perspective. God is an *effing* master planner and puzzle maker. There is so much going on here, all at the same time. I can't begin to explain it all. It's like an onion. Many layers. Every thing, everyone here, is exactly where they need to be, doing exactly what they need to do. All at the same time, it gives them a chance to be and do what they should."

I was trying to understand where I fit in all of this. "And, Azrael cares about the lambs because?"

"Azrael hasn't changed who he is. He cannot let go of his anger so he continues to store up the wrath that will come his way. He believes he is working God's will, but the reality is he offends God as much as those he torments. That crazy elk serves his purpose here. He thinks he is working his way back into God's graces and so until he does, he's trying to delay God's final judgment and wrath. He believes if he kills every lamb, sheep and ram sent here, the time for his judgment won't come, giving him more time to obtain redemption. He doesn't see it only serves to further seal his fate. He's blind to the word. He hasn't learned how to forgive. How to love. How to show mercy. But his time for judgment, like everyone else, will come."

"Well, that's some seriously flawed thinking."

"I didn't say it was rational. Only what it is."

Moriah started to bleat and wander around the barn. Every few seconds, she would return and rub against my leg, signaling it was time to pet her, or face her incessant bleating.

"We can't let that lunatic get her. No matter what."

"You mean that? Because you just might have to make that choice, you or her. You begged for an end to this not too long ago."

I looked down at Moriah and pictured them slaughtering her and hanging her up in this dead valley as some sick message, defying God.

"Screw that lunatic. I'm done killing and causing pain. My fate is what it is. What are we going to do?"

"There are a few options. None good. Eventually, Azrael and his army will come and they're not going to be happy. With either of us." He warned.

"And?"

"And, I suggest we go outside."

The darkness shrouding the countryside when we arrived was now swallowed by the light, revealing a small river behind the barn. Moriah and Zadkiel played, galloping about, chasing one another. I looked up to the sky and considered what came next. *Could we live in this place in perpetuity? If not, for how long could we survive here?* There is no doubt, eventually, Azrael will come for us. Even if this is the last place he'll search, he'll come. For the moment, I was healing and reveling in it. I realized that amidst the chaos of life, the tranquil peaceful spaces between the craziness, like this one, are the most treasured. I've come to see the gift of stringing together as many of those peaceful gaps in time as possible, in between the muck of life that inevitably hunts us down and finds us all, in between the torture. Had I only known, I would have focused more on those times.

The present gap was short lived. Zadkiel screamed. He bolted toward the river behind the barn. My heart jammed in my throat, I held my breath for a moment. *Had Azrael found us already?* I ran after Zadkiel and didn't see Moriah anywhere.

"What's wrong?" I yelled, chasing after him. "I thought we're supposed to be quiet!"

"Moriah fell in!"

I came to the edge of the river and saw the frenzied current carrying her away. She was paddling hard, but couldn't fight the pull of the water. I froze, momentarily, paralyzed. She looked back at us, helpless. She struggled to stay afloat. The voice inside my head shouted, *crunch time Louie, it's up to you or she's dead. Move!* I shook off the grip of shock and dove in. I swam as hard I could toward her. Zadkiel followed alongside on the land. Moriah kept bobbing above and below the surface. With great effort, and near complete exhaustion from fighting the current, I caught up to her. I reached out and managed to grab her leg. I pulled her close to me and kept her head above the surface. Zadkiel started to scream again. Initially, I couldn't hear him. The water roared and Moriah began bleating. I was trying to figure out how I would make it out of the river when I finally deciphered Zadkiel's screams.

"You've got to get out! There's a fall up ahead."

I knew I would survive the fall, but Moriah wouldn't. *The animals die here,* my mind cried. I saw Zadkiel run ahead and tilt his head so that his antlers jetted into the water. I back paddled, holding onto Moriah. We were picking up speed and only a few feet away from going over the side. I paddled as hard as I could, trying to get to the side. I had one shot at reaching him. I extended my arm trying to grab hold of one side of Zadkiel's antler, but lost my grip. I quickly recovered and grabbed the other side. This time I managed to hold on. The force tugged and pulled hard. Zadkiel stumbled. I thought we were going to pull him into the river with us. Instead, he regained his balance and began to back up, dragging us with him and pulling both of us out of the river. The magnificent antlers that had inspired me to shoot him, were the same antlers that now rescued us. A new wave of shame exploded through me.

I rolled over on my back. Moriah hobbled up to me and started to lick my face.

"Maybe there's hope for you." Zadkiel said, standing tall over me.

"Yeah, well, there's probably a thing or two I need to make up for. No big deal." I smiled, my chest still heaving from the strain.

The faint sounds of the horns wailed in the far distance, souring the moment.

"Listen. You hear that? They're coming for us, and I assume by now they know we're together. Judging the distance of that sound we don't have much time. If they suspect we've been helping to hide her," he said, turning to Moriah, "they're going to rain hell down upon us with such a ferocity you'll be begging to return to the torture you had been receiving before. I'm going to go lure them away."

"Not a chance." I rejected, springing to my feet.

Animal Killer

"I'll admit, it's not my first choice, but the decision was made the moment I uncrucified your ass. Now that the lamb is involved, we can't get caught. He'll never stop looking for her, or you. I'll lead him away from here, that'll give the two of you time to get away."

"No. There must be another way. Please. We won't survive without you." I pleaded, looking into his eyes.

"Yes you can," he softened his voice. "There's a place you can go. I didn't think you deserved to know about it. I'm still not entirely sure you do. I'd take the lamb myself, but I'm not sure how that scenario plays out with the Big Man. I'm not prepared to risk my redemption because I have doubts about you. I've done what I've done. Besides, I'm being practical. The three of us together get caught. The lamb and I together get caught. The only chance of escape is, I out run the army, they take the bait and follow me, you and Moriah get away. Simple."

"No. I won't let you do it. You take her and I'll distract the army."

"That won't work. You won't last long enough, and we both know you've exhausted your survival prowess. Head west. The road out of this perdition starts at the back of this valley. Follow it. Stay on the path. Don't stray. It'll lead you to *Discidium*.

It's no paradise, but those souls not destroyed here, are allowed to dwell there in limbo. At least you won't be hunted or tormented. You and Moriah go there. As long as you are with her, they'll let you in. It's your only option. When God is ready, He'll rescue the lamb."

"I really hate this idea." I protested.

"Louie!" He shouted firmly. "Keep it together. You should be thrilled, I just handed you a lifeline. Now promise me, you'll protect her. I don't know if she's the last one. No harm can come to her, no matter what. She can't be lost. No matter what, Louie. No matter what. Go, be free from this torment. If I can make it, I'll join you in *Discidium*, when it's safe."

The ground shook. Zadkiel and I looked at each other. No words were needed. They were in the valley of the rams and heading our way. The horns sounded again off in the distance, but this time closer. They came sooner than I hoped. There was no more time to debate what to do.

My life, at least what remained of it, had to find some modicum of meaning. So that was just what I would do. If Zadkiel was right about why Azrael and his army destroyed all the rams and sheep, she couldn't, shouldn't, die. I wouldn't allow it.

"Don't forget what I told you. You now know what you need to survive there. Follow the word, live a life of righteousness, and love freely. If you have those, you have everything. Got to go."

My heart sank. I didn't want to lose my new friend. I didn't want the responsibility of taking care of Moriah alone. Mostly, I did not want to find myself back on that cross.

"I'm out of here. See you around, dumbass." Zadkiel said and ran off.

"No! Zadkiel, don't go!" I shouted.

But he was gone. He darted off to meet the approaching army. Bait, to lure them away. I decided in that instant I would do what is right. I would take her to *Discidium*.

B. Lee Baker

The Eighteenth Chapter

Moriah and I moved quickly heading west, down the road leading out of perdition. My emotions battled. While I was distressed Zadkiel left us and would be caught, hope filled his absence. Learning there was a place I could hide, a sanctuary, buoyed my spirits. With each step farther away from Azrael, my hope grew. Hope that I might be spared from further torment. Hope that my genuine care and concern for Moriah might find some favor. Hope I would never meet the Spirit Destroyer. I was also confident Zadkiel would out smart Azrael and join us. The sting and constant call of hunger, thirst and cold gradually eased. And yet, I felt like I had made a cataclysmically bad decision letting Zadkiel go. He was the first genuine friend I had made in quite some time. It seems silly to admit, being I knew him so briefly. Another lesson learned after I had been stripped of everything, with nothing to lose and facing nothing but the darkness, the lesson of true friendship. The fact he is a deer makes the sentiment that much more absurd. But compared to the many fake friends I had made over the years, Zadkiel expressed more, taught more and done more for me in such a short time than the lifetime of the tenuous relationships I had formed. Unlike the gigantic farce that were the friends who scattered like shadows at twilight, Zadkiel rescued me from the abyss. He threw me a lifeline even though I shot him without the slightest concern. He was the living embodiment of true strength and forgiveness.

I continued looking back over my shoulder hoping to see Zadkiel galloping toward us, but he was nowhere to be seen. My concern for him continued to gnaw at me. I had never met anyone so willing to sacrifice and risk himself for others. Especially for someone who had wronged him the way I had. But, I remained hopeful. He was strong, fast and smart. He would guide them away from us and avoid capture. We would see each other again, and when we do, I will tell him how I felt, how his words and sacrifice helped change me. He gave me another chance. I would be different.

Then the screams started, distant and stifled, but carried by the wind. Moriah and I froze. The look we offered each other said it all. My foreboding and dread realized. Moriah knew something was wrong even if she was not sure exactly what it was. She was taking her cues from me and I did not want to alarm her. I did my best to remain calm and steady, but inside, my heart broke. A large lump clogged my throat. The hope and serenity I had been soaking in just a moment ago fled. *Those screams came from Zadkiel.* I was sure of it. *Why did I allow him to go?* He was so determined. The screams continued. Anxiety and consternation overwhelmed me. My breathing became more rapid and I started perspiring. I turned in the direction we had come, and thought about going back to try and help. He saved me. How could I just abandon him? I was torn, unsure what to do. I dropped to my knees and bowed my head. *What did God want me to do? What was the right thing?* I had gotten so much of my life so wrong, I no longer trusted my judgment. Moriah came to me and rubbed against my arm. Going back would mean certain death and destruction for me. I was powerless against them.

"Should I offer myself in his place? Maybe I can reason with Azrael and save you both. His and your life, for mine. What do you think?" I asked Moriah. Her expression remained unchanged blinking at me.

Sacrificing myself would mean leaving Moriah alone and taking an enormous risk. I did not believe Azrael would accept my life as a substitute for either Zadkiel or Moriah, let alone both. He was ruthless. *Once I got your ass, it ain't escaping.* I was reminded of Azrael's promise. Protecting Moriah was my priority which kept me from turning back. I convinced myself that this wasn't a lie I was telling myself. We all have our blind spots, impairing our ability to challenge the lies we tell ourselves. But, I believed, Azrael would send me to the Spirit Destroyer, kill Zadkiel and hunt down Moriah anyway. So unless I could rescue him, they were dead, and I would be destroyed. The only thing for me to do was to defer to Zadkiel's instructions. He made the decision before he left. He ordered me to stay and to protect Moriah at all costs. That was my charge. The debt I owed Zadkiel for my freedom. I would honor it no matter how difficult the choice.

I prayed, but, for only the second time in my life, I prayed for someone else. Sure, there had been times I prayed for some members of my family, but there was always some self interest in doing that. Praying for someone else, this was something new. First for the Joey, the Sport Hunter, now for Zadkiel. I didn't think God was listening to me, but I would try. *Please keep him safe. If he was caught, please ease his suffering. He has been through enough.*

Animal Killer

He saved me. He deserves to be saved. He offered me mercy. He deserves mercy. If that is not meant to be, please make it quick. Please reward him for his sacrifice. Take him to be with you into the Kingdom. I will miss him, but I can go in peace knowing he has been rewarded. Tell him dumbass says hello.

I pet Moriah to let her know everything was going to be okay. I smiled at her and stood. We continued west. The screams faded. We walked fast, without any rest. Despite my best efforts, Moriah seemed on edge, staying silent. I tried to lighten the mood by singing to her. In times of stress, I would dance and sing with my wife in the time before my son had been born. She loved Frank Sinatra. I learned all the songs she loved and would sing, decidedly off key, to her. It often worked, the stress usually melted away. So I decided to sing some Frank to Moriah.

It worked. Moriah began to purr bleats of contentment. I smiled, but below the surface, dread and Azrael stalked me. We continued walking west.

Singing to a lamb. Who am I? I thought to myself.

"Zadkiel will never tell them where we're headed, but eventually they will come. I am surprised we haven't even seen the bird squadron flying overhead. They must be out in force searching for us. It'll just be a matter of time. We should probably head for cover under some trees." I said, glancing skyward, hoping not to see any birds.

Moriah offered me a confused look and I laughed.

"You know. I have a confession. You remind me of a lamb I knew as a boy. Before my father taught me to hunt. I was so happy the day he brought him home. I had been asking for a dog. Leave it to my father to show up with a lamb. But, I was happy for the lamb. I was the only boy in the neighborhood with a pet lamb. I named him George. Then, with no warning, one day I came home from school and George was gone. I ran to my mother cooking in the kitchen. I asked her, momma, where is George? She crushed me, your father told you, but you would not listen. He is food, not a pet."

Moriah looked quizzically at me.

"Oh, I cried. No momma. No. George was my friend. Sad, huh?"

Just ahead, I could see a change in the landscape. A thin translucent membrane marked the boarder. It looked like floating water. This had to be *Discidium*.

"Look. Moriah, Look. We're almost there. We're going to make it. All of this is going to end."

I beamed with joy, for the first time in a long time, genuine hope presented itself to me. The nightmare was over. I ran toward the entryway. Moriah followed, galloping to catch up. I turned to make sure she followed. She looked so happy and thought we were playing. We were a few feet away, but I couldn't see beyond the boarder separating the two worlds.

I felt like a marathoner reaching the finish line. I stuck my chest out boldly as I crossed the threshold. Victory. A race well run and done. The light though on this side of the plane was strikingly dimmer. Several pale souls waited to greet me at the entrance.

"We made it Moriah." I shouted triumphantly.

Elation consumed me.

I turned, but Moriah was not there. My heart stopped. I raced toward the sheath separating me from Azrael's world of torment.

"Stop!" Shouted one of the pale faceless souls. "You cannot return if you leave. Stay or go. You cannot do both."

I put my face up to the sheath separating the two worlds, but could not see through. Stay and be free from the torment, or go. I had made so many bad choices. How could I go back and subject myself to the torment? How could I abandon Moriah when I made the promise to Zadkiel?

"Come on now. It's ok," the faces said to me, "You're safe here."

I waited several moments hoping she would step through. Panic strangled me. I cried out, "Moriah. Moriah." Nothing answered and she didn't step through. Something had gone wrong. Closing my eyes, I willingly leapt back to hell.

"Moriah!" I hollered.

She was gone. A hawk squawked from above, grabbing my attention. I looked upward and saw that he clutched Moriah in his talons. She cried and squirmed, but couldn't break free.

"Stop!" I shouted.

I ran after them. I was so fixated on following them, I didn't see Azrael and the animal army approaching ahead of me.

"Well, well, well. Wonders never do cease. Look at the Animal Killer making friends with the animals. You've really done it now. Now, you've got me mad. I told you there *ain't* no escaping." He said with a scowl.

Something hit me from behind and the world went dark.

I woke up disoriented. A stabbing pain quickly cleared the cloud and haze. I was back on my cross. Then, one singular thought screamed inside my head. *Moriah!* My heart throbbed. I looked to my right and was horrified to see Zadkiel strung up also. He was upside down, pinned to the cross previously occupied by the Sport Hunter. On the

Animal Killer

ground were Zadkiel's intestines, his blood pooled in the soil below. He was gone. The sign nailed to the cross above him read, "Traitor."

"You monster!" I shrieked.

Azrael stepped up to me and put his face up to mine.

"You've been a busy boy, Louie."

"Where is she?" I shouted.

"You mean the lamb?"

Two apes pushed and kicked Moriah and she stumbled and fell at my feet. She looked into my eyes.

"Stop this! Please, I beg you! I know who you are! Let it go! Lesson learned. I'm sorry. I'm not the same man. God doesn't want this. God wants you to let it go and forgive. He won't forgive you until you do! Repent and God will save you." I pled.

"Sport! Sounds like you did have your come to Jesus moment. Well, good for you. I never thought I'd see the day. Now, let's put it to the test. See if it– stuck, so to speak. What do *ya* think? I'll make you a deal. You were a lawyer, you know all about making deals, right, Louie? Here's my offer, I'll let you down and let you go. Right now, this very minute, all of this will end, you just have to do one small thing for me."

I was in agony. The spikes pinning me back to the cross renewed the job of destroying my soul. Zadkiel was dead. The torment was unbearable. The possibility of ending this sounded too good to be true. I had been so close to freedom, the feeling exacerbated the agony I now felt.

"What's that? Anything!" I shouted.

"Anything? Okay, Animal Killer. I'll let you down right now, you just have to kill the lamb. Easy, right?"

I should have known this beast would never offer me any real redemption.

"We'll have us a real nice cookout. Lamb chops. I know you've been hungry. What do *ya* say?" He said, grinning wide.

My pain was so great, I could hardly understand his words. I desperately wanted out of this hell. I couldn't bear another minute of torture. My mind reeled. I didn't know what to do. I didn't know what to say. He motioned to the apes who removed me from the cross. The agony instantly subsided. *I could be free from this*, was my pervading thought. Every ounce of my being screamed to be free.

"Go on sport. Wouldn't be the first time for you."

One of the apes threw a knife that landed perfectly at my feet, imbedding itself into the ground, blade first. Moriah scurried over to me and was now rubbing against my leg.

Just get it over with, something within me cried.

Azrael stepped close to me.

"Come on Louie. You've been begging for mercy. Here it is. She's dead either way. Might as well save yourself."

My mind raced and my breath quickened. My thoughts bounced between Fate and Free Will, both so clearly at work. The Deciders unmistakably taught me that both do in fact exist at the same time. I had always believed I could be brave when needed, but when confronting the demon face to face and the rubber met the road, I found myself cracking.

I grabbed the knife.

I had committed to protect this lamb, but failed. *What would be the point in my continued suffering as well?* I reasoned.

"Crunch time, sport." Azrael prodded.

I leaned over, the knife in one hand, I pet Moriah with the other. Time to decide.

Then, with no warning, I lunged toward Azrael.

He and the apes were ready. I never really had a chance and didn't come close to striking him. Azrael leapt sideways as the apes simultaneously grabbed me from behind. His all-powerful grip squeezed and the knife fell from my hand.

"Big mistake, you little piss-ant. I don't know what that traitor said to change you," he said disgusted, motioning toward Zadkiel's mutilated carcass still rotting on the cross next to me, "but whatever it was, too little, way too late, as far as I am concerned. And, one more piece of advice, next time you consider preaching, focus on your own salvation, and I'll worry about mine."

I turned my attention to Moriah, we locked eyes, expecting the worst.

"No matter what they do, it's going to be ok. I tried. I really, really tried. I'm so sorry, we were so close. I'm sorry I failed." I wept.

Azrael nodded, it happened in slow motion and yet in an instant, one of the apes retrieved the fallen knife.

"*Noooooo!!!*" I shouted.

The brute bent down and cut Moriah's throat in the swift fluid motion of an experienced executioner. Blood squirted from her and splashed me across my face with a slap. It stained her spotless white coat. I watched her fade away, as she never turned her gaze from me.

My mouth opened to scream, but nothing came out. I screamed without a sound being made.

When there was nothing left to her, they dragged Moriah away. I assumed they were bringing her back to the valley of the rams. I wanted no more. I could not stand anymore. I could not withstand the murder of another innocent life. It was an assaulting holocaust upon my soul. No being was meant to endure all I had been forced to experience. It was the last act needed for the total destruction and annihilation of my spirit. My mind closed off and I withdrew into depths of despair I had not known existed.

"He's done." Azrael proclaimed.

My mind shut off. I barely felt or noticed that they dragged me to the opposite side of the cross I had previously been attached, and reaffixed me back to it. I was now facing the wall. The home of the Spirit Destroyer. They blew the ram's horns, but this time, the sound boomed in a very low, vibrating, octave. Two apes pounded on the bronze doors. Then, they all ran. For the first time, they looked scared. Moments later the doors burst open. It felt like a giant vacuum turned on. Everything was being sucked inside his lair. The force was so intense, it pulled me out from the depths from where I had retreated. As the pressure increased, the metal spikes pinning me to my cross began to pry free. The force so powerful, it sucked the air out of my lungs and tugged at my eyeballs, pulling at them in their sockets.

I realized the end was here. By God's design, these were to be my last moments before the final bludgeoning and my total destruction. I would never have a thought again. I was headed for Oblivion. I am proud to say in the face of indescribable terror and torment, I had no regrets refusing to sell out and destroy Moriah to save myself. It might have taken more than an entire lifetime to learn, but I learned. I learned to love genuinely, not conditionally, and I did love Moriah. Learning to love a little thing that couldn't do a thing for me. Now, that was something. I would have gladly traded my life for Moriah's, or Zadkiel's, had that been possible. I would have been at peace knowing I would had done one truly consequential thing in my life, but that wasn't to be. It would have served as some small measure of redemption. Of all the things I could die for, or be killed for, dying to protect her, there was no cause more worthy or noble.

As the spikes loosened, I took my final moments to think of my prior life. My family. All the wrong. All the mistakes. Things I should have known. Things I had been told, but ignored. Things that had been laid out before me, but I had remained willfully blind to, just to fit in, to be like everyone else. To live the life I thought I was meant to live. All the damage I had caused to so many of God's beings. I knew my end was just. I accepted that I had never really done anything of value with my existence until this very moment. My victories and defeats. What did it all mean? I had screwed it all up. I could not tell my friends or family how I loved them. Even my wife, whom I did love very much, had to bear the burdens of me. She had to compromise and make enormous sacrifices to keep the peace. I had been a hard man to like. The few sacrifices I had made, too inconsequential to mention. All I had acquired meant nothing. It was all gone. It was all borrowed and meant nothing at this moment.

But I believe, in my final moments, I had accomplished something of immense consequence. God opened my heart and gifted me a glimpse of unconditional and unbounded love, before He would destroy me. Rather than turning away, I embraced it, loving Moriah and Zadkiel. Not love for two animals, but love for a friend, love for an innocent being trying to navigate the challenging tribulations of life. In the end, love for God through His creations. As all humans yearn, Moriah and Zadkiel longed to be free from pain, free from persecution. With that revelation, the Animal Killer became the Animal Lover, and I was quite alright with that. The sad thing though, Azrael was right, it was too little, too late. There are consequences to living a life littered with sin. The evil one waiting on the other side of the door would not be denied.

With a final tug, the spikes gave way. For the first time since arriving here, I felt full, my thirst had been quenched and my chill warmed. I flew through the open doors and into the arms of the Spirit Destroyer. As I crossed the threshold I felt my skin pull from my bones. I looked up, however, and smiled, offering my last prayer and plea to God.

"Thank you for revealing the truth. I know her death wasn't the end. That is my solace. Protect her and give her a good life; that is all I ask. I am ready, and I am sorry."

The Last Chapter

I was back on the platform in the arena sitting in the accused's chair. My presence made no sense to me. I was disoriented and dazed. It took a moment for my eyes to adjust and process my continued survival and the scene before me. Through the fog and uncertainty, I was aware that something was measurably different. I was alive, whatever that really meant. The thunderous cries and screams and sounds that previously reverberated throughout the colosseum were now gone, replaced by total quiet, a negative silence. As the haze lifted, I surveyed the millions of eyes studying me. Instead of the angry pleas for justice which had been shouted toward me, no one made a sound. Not a whisper or an echo. *Had I survived the Spirit Destroyer, escaped Oblivion, was I going back?* I turned and saw the Deciders standing, staring back at me. Their faces offered nothing. Even Saint Francis stood with an unblinking fixated stare. Surely he would have something to say. I waited for an insult or damning accusation. None came. He offered nothing. Karma stood next to me. I was thoroughly confused.

Before all of this, I didn't know if God actually existed. I never admitted that to anyone. Deep down, I periodically considered that there were only one of three possibilities: One, that there is no God. Two, that there is a God, but He cannot help. Or, three, and possibly worst of all, there is God, but He refused to help, that He had turned His back on us. I accepted this last option as the most plausible. Who could blame Him for abandoning us? We had all turned our backs on Him first, a long, long, time ago. None of these possibilities comforted me. But I now know the truth. God has given us what we need to gain peace and happiness and wellness. It comes down to whether we want to accept or reject His gifts. We are all things, kind and cruel, good and bad, saint and sinner. It simply comes down to what we choose. The choice is ours. Always had been.

My mind suddenly shifted as I thought of Zadkiel and Moriah. I leapt out of my chair, my heart pounding. Their loss and the sudden memory of their massacres sickened me. Profound sadness and loss consumed me. I was alone once again, facing those responsible for sending me to Hell.

Karma leaned over and grabbed my arm.

"Take a moment."

I felt unsteady and thought I was going to vomit and pass out.

He spoke, "It is done."

Still grasping my arm, he guided me down the stairs of the platform. He moved me toward the doorway I had entered and exited once before. The place remained completely silent.

Had I just imagined those events? Was I heading now to serve my sentence and had just experienced a foreshadowing of what was to come? I needed answers.

"Wait. What happened to Zadkiel and Moriah?" I demanded.

Karma looked at me.

"Well?"

"Come with me," he said, guiding me.

"I want to know what happened to them! Where are they? Haven't I suffered enough? Please tell me. I did all I could to save her." I shouted.

Silence continued to grip the arena. Karma grabbed me by the wrist, like a child being pulled through the supermarket. He was so strong, I could not free myself or resist. The millions of onlookers remained absolutely still and silent, observing the spectacle.

"*Noooo!*" My shout echoed.

I fell to the ground, but he continued to drag me. Karma faced the door with his back to me as he pulled me along. His cruel indifference refused to satiate my desire to know. All I wanted was to know what had happened to them.

"All I can tell you is that you've got to go through that door, now. There can be no delay once the decision is made."

"I want to go back. Give me another chance. I repent! I am sorry. Let me go back. I will do all I can. Please tell me how they are! I did what I could," I begged, as I tried to stop his progress.

Neither Karma nor the multitudes would share a thing. The place echoed with my pleas. I pledged that if I was returned and given another chance, I would with all my heart, and all my mind, use all my money, all my resources, and devote all my time to saving all those I could. I promised to protect those who cannot protect themselves. Nothing convinced Karma to stop. He continued to pull me closer to the door. All I could hope is that when I go through the door, it would be the last time. I could not endure any more. I was drained physically, emotionally, spiritually.

I didn't know what awaited me on the other side of the door. I hoped to see my friend Zadkiel again. I hoped I would see Moriah and sing to her and hold her and protect her. I also hoped Moriah recognized that even though we knew each other for such a short time, I had come to love her very much. She rescued me from the abyss. And, I hoped to see all those who loved me, and all those I loved.

I longed for someone to comfort me, to tell me it's all over, to tell me to be at peace. To tell me I had atoned and that I am loved. That I can now rest, but I didn't see any of that happening. I even hoped Azrael made it. I hoped he learned, or would learn to forgive. I wanted to see him, to tell him I forgave him, the way Zadkiel had forgiven me. Life can be so hard. It is so easy to get lost. Evil stalks us, but we can and must resist. Resist the calling to follow and keep from falling into that pit. And, if we do tumble in, to fight it, to climb out and turn away from the darkness.

I didn't know how this would all end, but one thing I did know, I was ready to be a warrior for God if given the opportunity. I would love all He created and would work tirelessly to protect it. I hoped that I had atoned, even if I had failed.

I accepted that what would be, would be. And, even if I had done too little too late and was headed to Oblivion, at least before my time was up, I saw the light. I got a glimpse of what could be. What should be. At least where I was once blind, I now could see. Karma tapped the door. It opened and I stepped through at peace.

The End.

-SDG

About The Author

B. LEE BAKER, is a practicing attorney in New Jersey and New York. Over the last decade he spent much of his spare time assisting others on the front lines feeding, transporting, helping and finding homes for countless animals in need. *Animal Killer* is his first novel.

Made in the USA
San Bernardino, CA
09 December 2019